Countess Chronicles #2

The Duchess Wager

Katherine Grant

Cover design by Julia Gerbach
Book interior design by Asya Blue

ISBN 978-1-7343813-3-7 (paperback)
ISBN 978-1-7343813-4-4 (ebook)

www.katherinegrantromance.com

Praise for *The Ideal Countess*, Book 1 of The Countess Chronicles series

If you enjoy a good Regency romance with characters that will pull on your heart strings and a plot that is different than so many historical romances, then you will enjoy *The Ideal Countess* as much as I did. I'm amazed by the talent in this debut novel and will be looking for more books by Katherine Grant. Happy reading!

— Vikki Vaught (Romance Writer and Reviewer)

The Ideal Countess is a stunning regency debut, with strong-willed characters that set their sights with determined precision.

— Nicole Highland (Romance Writer and Reviewer)

This story is a masterpiece at developing the main character from a naive debutant to a mature, self-aware woman. This is one of those books that I highly recommend reading in one sitting. I loved being able to lose myself in the story.

— Melissa from Probably at the Library
(*Regency Romance Book Reviewer*)

January 3, 1811

My dear Alice,

I can hear you gasping in shock: I have not married Lord Gresham, after all!

I know you are clamoring to hear what happened, so the short of it is this: a certain Duchess of Surrey returned to Ambley Park just before the wedding to reunite with her first and true love – none other than my intended, Lord Gresham! Seeing that she had a greater claim to his heart than I did, I wished them well as they headed north to Gretna Green. I daresay they may visit you at Bleneccle Manor, and you must not be scandalized that the new Lady Gresham is not me!

For now, know that I am still your Miss Lisbeth Dawes, unmarried, and rather happily so, I must admit.

Rather than dwell on the topic, I redirect your attention to a more pressing question. I read of a fire set by Luddites at a cotton mill in Shropshire, not far from your own sister Margot's home. Is she still safe and sound at Bleneccle Manor with you?

Your dear friend,

Miss Lisbeth Dawes

Chapter One

Somewhere between Gretna Green and Carlisle, Fitz concluded he had left lovely Earth and descended straight to Hell.

How else could one explain being trapped in a carriage – not even his own – with two newlyweds who wouldn't stop pawing each other?

Of course, he'd always imagined Hell a bit warmer than the frigid January air of Northern England. This must be a special torment reserved for dukes like him: to freeze eternally while watching his once-rational best friend offer endless hand rubs to his new wife.

"Only you could look so adorable with a red nose," Annabelle, the new Lady Gresham, cooed.

"The worst winter in Cumberland couldn't make you any less a goddess," Talbot responded, in a tone Fitz had never heard from his friend before embarking on this damned adventure with the couple.

There had been six Dukes of Harrodshire before Fitz, and surely, none of them had been stupid enough to help their best friend elope.

He'd been happily enjoying the house party to ring in the New Year and celebrate Talbot's upcoming marriage to a Miss Dawes when Talbot's long-lost love Annabelle, the Duchess of Surrey, had arrived from the Continent with the news that she was now a widow. Stunning everyone, Talbot had thrown Miss Dawes aside to elope with the duchess in Gretna Green at the Scottish border.

Fool that he was, Fitz had agreed to accompany them. Not that Talbot needed anyone to stand up with him in the elopement town. Fitz was only there to facilitate the next part of the happy couple's journey: to announce the marriage to the new Duke of Surrey. Annabelle's stepson, fifteen years older than she, had never favored his stepmother, and she feared he would refuse her the settlement his father had promised her. Since Fitz was unluckily the fellow's cousin – perhaps, too, because Fitz was known around town as the Diplomatic Duke – they hoped his presence would lessen the shock of the scandal to Annabelle's former family.

When he agreed, Fitz had pictured himself making the journey on his trusty mare, Roona, rather than ensconced in the marital coach. But he wasn't accustomed to the whistling wind on the Cumbrian mountain passes. He'd decided a few hours ago that being stuck with lovebirds was preferable to freezing to death atop his steed.

He was beginning to think he'd chosen wrong.

It wasn't that Fitz objected to Talbot's newfound happiness; nor did he consider marriage a foolish occupation. It was that the carriage reeked of emotion. On their side it was an overbearing perfume of joy, love, desire, humor, and hope. As for Fitz, soon he was going to have to admit to one or two emotions of his own. Which was precisely what he objected to.

"Do you think there's going to be a storm?" Lady Gresham asked, peeling her eyes from Talbot for the first time in ages to peek behind the window curtain "It's so very gray."

Talbot rubbed her palms more vigorously. "You've been gone too long, my dear. England is always gray."

Fitz's knee had ached all day from an old injury, as it usually did when buckets of precipitation approached. And he'd been watching the clouds as they swelled dark along the edges, as if smudged with angry charcoal.

"The maid at the inn this morning told me it would snow today," Lady Gresham protested. "Perhaps we should find a place to stay, rather than get stuck on the road in a flurry."

Talbot opened his mouth, then closed it again. He turned to Fitz. "Where are we anyway?"

"Lake District. Passed Carlisle an hour ago or so."

"Say we can stop in the nearest town," Lady Gresham pressed. "I do hate to feel exposed in a carriage in bad weather. Anything can happen."

Talbot, predictably, melted. "Of course, my darling."

Fitz grimaced. Staying in town meant another night squeezing into whatever accommodations the local inn could provide. In Gretna Green – overcrowded that first week of January with elopers – the newlyweds had gotten a suite while he'd been relegated to a hatbox above the stables on a mattress stuffed with moldy straw. He could only imagine what a small town on the little-used northern roads would offer up.

"We are nearing the seat of the Baron of Eastley. Perhaps this is a good time to pay a visit..." As he suggested this, Fitz raised his eyebrow in what he knew to be an intimidating gesture. Most of the time, the ducal eyebrow incited immediate action, a scurrying out of his way, even a gasp every now and then.

Lady Gresham – who, to be fair, had herself been a duchess until the day before – merely summoned a smile of delight in response. "Perfect. We can wait out the storm among friends."

It was the lesser of two evils. Fitz hated imposing unexpectedly on others of the *ton* only slightly less than he hated being stuck with his present traveling companions. He knew next to nothing about the Baron of Eastley, other than that he was getting along in years, had two married daughters instead of a direct heir, and lived at a seat somewhere up in these forsaken northern counties. Rapping on the ceiling of the coach, he braved the cutting wind to arrange with the driver – nearly a human icicle – to go directly to the baron's Bleneccle Manor, as soon as they could figure out where it was.

"I don't know what we'd do without you, Your Grace," Lady Gresham cooed as they pressed onward.

He knew what he'd do without *them*. For one thing, he'd already be warm and snug at his favored Pembroke Abbey on the southern coast. He'd likely be reviewing the accounts with his steward, or riding the grounds, or perhaps holed up in his study with a snifter of brandy to work on his three proposed reforms for the Parliamentary season.

He wouldn't be counting the bumps in the road that stood between him and a nice hot fire.

"I suppose you could do without us, eh?" Talbot picked up the response, ears reddening as if he were only now realizing their behavior. "Perhaps we'd better engage in civilized conversation for a bit, light of my life."

Lady Gresham obligingly slid into her own seat. "Yes, let us turn the conversation to our honorable companion. You've never been married, Your Grace?"

This not being the first time he'd been quizzed by a female on his marital plans, Fitz knew he had two options: change the subject or entertain the topic long enough to satisfy her curiosity.

He attempted the first. "Call me Fitz. After this trip, we surely must be close enough to use Christian names."

"Then I am Annabelle." She smiled, running her eyes appraisingly across his face. "You are not yet married, but you must be close to thirty if not over it now. It is getting to be the prime age to begin the business of heirs."

The first option having proved ineffective, Fitz supposed he could stand to indulge the lady's interest. "You are astute. I suppose this Season or next, I'll walk away with a bride. However, I have exacting tastes, particularly when it comes to my future duchess. Not just any debutante will do."

"Let me guess," Talbot drawled. "You have a list of requirements drawn up in the care of your undersecretary. She must be beautiful, intelligent, equal parts haughty and approachable, appropriately interested in politics, and not too invested in receiving your attention."

Fitz offered a laugh at his own expense, though Talbot's comment was a little too close to the mark for his comfort. He had never written down a list, never discussed it with a member of his staff, yet certainly he had decided on the features that would make his duchess successful. And Talbot had listed most of them.

"You expect to find all those qualities in an innocent debutante?" Annabelle raised her golden eyebrows in doubt. "Sometimes I wonder how we expect our young ladies to be ready for marriage at the tender age of twenty when we fully anticipate the young gentlemen needing another decade to ripen."

An astute comment, one Fitz hadn't expected from a woman renowned primarily for her likeness to Venus.

"And what of affection?" she continued. "If not love, don't you wish for some sort of mutual affection between yourself and your wife?"

"I imagine that should I meet a young lady whose qualities are those I seek, affection will arise naturally, given that she is everything I desire."

Annabelle narrowed her eyes at him. Fitz felt for a moment that she could see straight through his words to the smooth surface of his heart; that she could measure every dalliance he'd had with actresses, his muddy affairs with bored wives, even the boyhood crushes he'd bestowed upon debutantes and neighborhood ladies, and in all of them found him lacking.

The bewitchment ended as quickly as it had begun. Annabelle turned to her husband, the pink of excitement on her cheeks. "My intuition tells me his fate will be different from these well-laid plans. I think we should challenge His Grace to a wager."

Talbot, rather than looking shocked, smiled wickedly. "And what would that wager be?"

"Fifty pounds that he will meet a new sweetheart in the next three months and *she* will be the woman he marries."

Now Talbot frowned. "In the next three months? That's rather specific, don't you think?"

Annabelle waved it off. "If my intuition is correct, it won't even be that long before his heart belongs to another."

In the next three months, Fitz planned to be fully ensconced in Parliamentary agenda – after all, the Prince Regent needed installation, in addition to the reforms Fitz hoped to pass – not meeting young ladies. The wager was a woman's folly.

Talbot turned to him. "What do you say?"

Fitz spread his palms in the air. "The whole purpose of my accompanying you on this trip is to help you secure a fortune, not to take it away from you."

"Oh fie, this is more fun," Annabelle cried. "Besides, we'll win."

She was so certain, though logic decreed she would fail. Fitz wondered for a moment if she perhaps had a more powerful intuition than most. But he shook himself free of the thought; he didn't lend credence to superstition. He alone controlled his fate, and he had no plans to fall in love, much less marry whatever poor creature could capture his heart. "Make it a hundred pounds, and you have a deal."

Though he blanched at the sum, Talbot shook his hand to make the wager official.

Fitz grinned. "I look forward to collecting from you at my wedding, which will be to some young lady whom I *won't* meet in the next three months."

"And I look forward to watching you tumble desperately into love," Annabelle rejoined.

By now, the carriage had jostled off the turnpike down a forested road. Flurries swirled around the carriage amidst a darkened sky, so Fitz could make out Bleneccle Manor only in bits and pieces as they drew closer. The gray stone fence. Wrought iron gate. A turreted tower looming above the drive. And then the orange glow of candles in the windows.

At least someone was home.

"What an adventure," Annabelle crooned as the carriage came to a stop.

Her enthusiasm was infectious. Fitz was too tall to sit compressed in a carriage on the best of days; the cold only made him feel worse, as if he'd been bound by ropes all day. His rear end pulsed in pain as blood started rushing there again. Every bone ached. His fingers and toes were positively numb.

And yet his heart thrummed with the same excitement as Annabelle's. *What an adventure.*

Chapter Two

Margot did not want to awaken from her afternoon nap. Her bed was cozy, the woolen blanket cocooned around her and the curtains tied shut so she could pretend the whole world existed within her four-poster canopy. With her eyes closed, Margot didn't have to worry about what time of day it was, or whether the children were arguing, or about catching one of those terrible, pitying looks from her family.

If only she could stay asleep, still in dreamland, she might stay at peace.

But alas, she was awake. Even as she contemplated a blissful future of endless sleep, her eyes popped open, as if to announce, *Time to get up!*

Groaning, she rolled toward the edge of the mattress and peeked out from the curtains. The room was too bright for her sleepy eyes. Someone had added coal to her fire and lit the candles near her dressing table. Moreover, outside the afternoon sky was so dark that the glass windowpanes reflected all the light right back in.

She hadn't meant to sleep *that* late.

A shout tore through the room: "Mama! Mama is awake!" And then came the ferocious pitter patter as her son George, the Earl of Wickham, raced to the bed. Never mind the knot keeping the curtain panels closed: he found a way around them and mounted the mattress like a knight scaling the enemy's castle. Trailing him came Valentina, Margot's two-year-old, clutching her doll as she tried to repeat George's words.

"It's snowing, Mama! Nurse says we can play in it when the storm ends. The wind is noisy. Valentina got scared and cried."

Margot put on a smile as George bounced around the bed giving his reports, his four-year-old energy too vast to be limited by the small space of a mattress. She grabbed ahold of him as he started jumping up and down, lest he land on her knee or ankle, and sat him in her lap. "Did you give Valentina a kiss to cheer her up?"

He scowled. "Nurse made me."

"There's a good brother."

The bed curtains parted for good and Margot's sister, Alice, lifted Valentina to join them on the bed. Now expecting her own first child, Alice was particularly keen to help with her niece and nephew. "How was your nap?"

Nestling Valentina next to her, Margot tried to convince her sister with one smile that everything was all right. "Very restful, thank you."

Alice's green eyes studied her suspiciously. Five years Margot's junior, Alice was usually the one being taken care of, not the other way around. But ever since Geoff had died – no, ever since Margot had retreated home to Bleneccle Manor to lick her wounds – their roles had been reversed. Now Margot was the fragile one, and Alice was the one doing the worrying.

Margot wished it weren't so.

George pounded her shoulder for attention. "Mama, there are visitors here, too. Grandmama said I could have a snow battle with them tomorrow. May I? May I leave Valentina behind? She'll only cry, and these are real men."

Valentina, sensing her good name was being dragged through the mud, squawked in protest from the safety of Alice's arms.

How Margot longed to turn back time by just a few minutes. Sleep had been so peaceful. Even *she* hadn't bothered herself while sleeping.

But there was no use wishing and hoping for the impossible. She was no more going to get peace than Geoff was going to return from the dead. She turned to Alice, planning to ask after the visitors, yet what erupted from her lips was, "Oh, I'm sick to my teeth of this!"

Even the children were silent for a moment, shocked still at the desperation flooding her tone. Surprise and dismay danced across Alice's face. Then she marshaled a sympathetic smile. "You've been out of sorts for so long, Margot. Perhaps we can think of something that will lift your spirits."

"You've been here a month doing nothing but that," Margot grumbled. "I know you and Hugh would have left for Richmond Hall weeks ago if you weren't whispering with Mother about how I'm not coping well. Yet nothing helps, does it? Not games of charades, nor wassailing, nor riding in the country. Not sleeping; not waking. I'm a useless bag of gloom."

Alice intercepted George as he was about to bludgeon Margot again for attention; sending him on a mission to the nursery to choose the toys he would take out in the snow, she turned back to Margot. "No one is whispering about you or calling you useless. You lost your husband suddenly. Of course you are overwhelmed."

They'd said as much to her before, and it didn't help. She hadn't loved Geoff the way her family thought she had, not for years, not since he'd relegated her to the role of country wife. He was her provider, the father of her children, a seasonal companion, an occasional thorn in her side. She missed him, but more than that, she resented his absence.

Still, she couldn't confess to such feelings, not to her family.

"Hugh loved his mother just as much, and he isn't moping," Margot said instead, referring to Alice's husband, whose mother had died just after the harvest.

"That's different." Sighing, Alice set Valentina on the floor and took Margot's hand instead. "You're being stubborn."

This, from Alice, was the pot calling the kettle black. Though Margot could admit that Alice had learned the trait honestly from her, and she in turn had learned it from their father, Reginald Winpole, Baron of Eastley.

Just as Margot was about to respond — with something

childish, like "Am not" – Alice smiled, the cat that ate the canary. "How's this, Countess of Contrary? I'd like to make you a wager that you will *not* be in better spirits by the end of the week."

"You would bet against your own sister's happiness?" Margot was interested enough to raise an eyebrow. "What will you win when I am still this cesspool of despondence?"

Alice tapped her chin in thought. "If I win – and you are still describing yourself in such morose terms at the end of this very week – you will, when addressing me, call me 'Your Loveliness, My Superior Sister in Every Way.' For the rest of the month."

"Your Loveliness, My Superior Sister." The words tasted like bilge on her tongue.

"In Every Way," Alice prodded.

Margot could see what Alice was about, and as much as she didn't appreciate being managed like a toddler, she had to admit it was working. "And what would I win, if I am suddenly as bright as a spring morning come Sunday?"

Alice's hands landed on her stomach. "You may name my firstborn child."

An enticing prize. Margot immediately started a mental list of names that she knew her sister hated. She wouldn't be so evil, of course – the poor child would have to live with whatever fate Margot handed it – but it would be fun to torment Alice with possibilities.

"You have a wager, dear sister who is not my superior." She sealed the deal with a kiss to Alice's cheek. "In fact, I am already feeling better. Well enough to face these visitors, anyway. Who are they? Stragglers in the storm?"

"The Duke of Harrodshire and the new Lord and Lady Gresham, seeking refuge from the snow." Blond and pale, Alice was cursed with every emotion racing across her face the instant she felt it, and now her face flashed with anger. "On their way south from Gretna Green."

Margot echoed Alice's anger immediately. Lord Gresham had been engaged to their friend, Miss Lisbeth Dawes, only to jilt her on the very day of their wedding to elope with the former Duchess of Surrey instead.

They'd just received Miss Dawes's letter, which tried so very hard to explain the thing away as mutually beneficial, when really it was the scandal of the decade.

And now the terrible Lord Gresham and his equally terrible new bride were here. At Bleneccle Manor. Their guests.

"And we received them?" Margot asked.

Alice raised her chin, a clear expression of disagreement. "Mother said it wouldn't be charitable to turn them away in this weather, no matter the scandal. Besides, Father didn't want to offend the Duke of Harrodshire."

"What are we supposed to do, play parlor games with the man who broke Miss Dawes's heart?"

Alice shrugged, scooping up Valentina again before the girl raced straight into the fire. "Mother asks that we be gracious hostesses as always. Apparently, it's not our battle."

Margot snorted. In many ways, she and her mother, Lady Sybil Eastley, were similar: it was from her that Margot inherited her dark hair, brown eyes, and hopeless love of sweets. But her mother was a gentle woman who loved long chats over hot tea, who always assumed the best of all humanity, and who avoided conflict at all costs.

Margot far preferred the thrill of getting her way, especially these days, when the burn of anger replaced the infinite black depths that hung about her heart.

"Besides, the Duke of Harrodshire is apparently influential in getting Father's canal built, so we mustn't offend him," Alice added.

A hot swell of anger steamed from deep within Margot's stomach. Father with his canal was getting to be as bad as Geoff had been with his damned mill. She snickered. "Didn't Hugh say Father's money would be better spent on a railroad, anyway?"

That earned a sly smile from her sister, who particularly loved it when Margot quoted Alice's new husband back to her.

Ringing for her maid, Margot reclaimed Valentina, stamping her with a great big mother's kiss. Then she shooed her down the hall to the playroom, where Nurse was waiting.

"What we need is a strategy," she announced to Alice. "One that allows us to always remain on Miss Dawes's side without offending Mother or risking Father's precious canal."

Her sister leaned against the bed, one hand resting thoughtfully on her increasing stomach. "What exactly do you have in mind?"

Margot flung open her wardrobe. It was full of black, of course, but still, there were options. Ever since Geoff had died – taken by an infection after slicing his hand while surveying his precious cotton mill – she'd only worn the comfortable black dresses. But the dressmaker had provided her with a full retinue of widow's weeds, including a few for the latter stages of grief that were grayer and more daring.

More distracting.

Margot turned to Alice, a slow bubble of excitement expanding in her chest. "You'll make it clear to Lord and Lady Gresham exactly whose side we're on. Meanwhile, I will occupy the Duke of Harrodshire, so he doesn't ever notice."

Alice grinned. "I had better watch out, otherwise you'll be winning this wager before the week even ends."

Chapter Three

Bleneccle Manor, Fitz decided, was warmer than it appeared. Given its stony walls and high ceilings, dark shadows tended to amass in the corners of the great hall, the corridor, even his bedroom. The tapestries were all threadbare and stained from too many years' use, and there were so many fires and candles burning that Fitz had the sensation his white gloves would be gray before the night was over.

Yet the whole place thrummed with some greater glow. The whistling wind outside didn't penetrate the castle, so Fitz was quite comfortable in his regular dress coat and had no need to huddle close to a fire to warm his hands. The servants had ready smiles, even a few jokes, as they settled him in. And it helped that the guest apartment they showed him to was more than an improvement over some little town inn. Fitz had a two-room suite featuring a goose-feather mattress, a roaring fire, a private cabinet of brandy, and a whole shelf of books ranging from agriculture to sciences to philosophy.

He would be quite happy to spend the whole evening alone in his room. Alas, the one downside of staying with the *ton*: he was expected to socialize with his hosts.

Dinner was impressively formal, given that Lady Eastley's guests had shown up unexpectedly in the middle of a snowstorm. Fitz reported to the drawing room to find a veritable crowd. Talbot and Annabelle were already cozying up on a narrow settee near the fireplace, chatting with their host. Lord Eastley himself took up a lot of space, both physically – for he was tall and wide – and energetically, as he spoke from the diaphragm and tended to thunder with laughter after every comment.

Lady Eastley, a much slimmer and calmer profile, stood near the corner window with another couple. Fitz recognized Lord Hugh Osborne, Earl of Windemere, from the thick set of spectacles sliding down his nose. The blonde sparkling at his side, Fitz concluded, was his new wife and daughter to the Winpoles, Lady Alice.

"Excuse me, Your Grace." The words came from behind. Fitz turned to discover he'd been blocking the threshold for yet another member of the party. This woman, he was sure, he'd never met before in his life.

In looks, she bore a passing resemblance to Lady Eastley. Dark, demure hair framed a wide forehead, slender eyebrows, and soft, supple lips. Her charcoal mourning gown scooped around her neckline to set off creamy skin and suggest a generous hourglass shape. A diamond pendant sparkled deliciously near to her bosom.

Fitz stepped aside, bowing his head as he did so. She responded with a curtsy, then rustled by, exuding the soft smell of rose water as she passed.

Fitz took a slow, steady breath. Perhaps Annabelle had been right about one part of the wager: he *would* meet his next sweetheart soon.

"Papa, I don't believe I've been introduced to all our guests," the widow said. Fitz was delighted to discover she spoke in low, throaty tones.

Lord Eastley rose to do his duty. "I believe you know Lord Gresham, and may I present the new Lady Gresham."

The widow curtsied again. "We were prepared to offer our felicitations to our dear friend Miss Dawes, but I see the plan changed."

If Fitz had been sipping a drink, he would have spurted it out. Talbot looked as if he'd seen a ghost, and even Annabelle had the good sense to blush.

"May you have a long and happy marriage," the widow said, turning away.

Turning towards him.

Lord Eastley cleared his throat. "And this is His Grace Lord Haight, Duke of Harrodshire. My daughter, Countess of Wickham."

That made her Geoff Wharton's widow. Fitz had known the man only nominally, since Wharton had, for the most part, ignored his duties as a member of the House of Lords. Fitz had heard of Wharton's sudden death over the summer, but he hadn't felt the need to travel to the funeral.

"Friends call me Fitz," he said, bowing at the introduction.

Lady Wickham's eyes teased him. "I shall remember that should I meet one of your friends."

They observed a half hour of socializing before the

butler announced that dinner was served. To Fitz's chagrin, Lady Wickham's playful eyes remained firmly away from him. While her mother seized his arm and begged for news of London, Lady Wickham joked with Osborne, smiled indulgently at her sister, and even slipped in a few more speared words toward Talbot and Annabelle. Once, as he bemoaned with Lady Eastley just how hard the roads were between Carlisle and London, Fitz thought he felt Lady Wickham's thoughtful gaze, but when he turned – pretending to reach for his sherry – he saw only her back.

A beautiful, graceful back, from the slender neck down to the soft, shapely waist.

"It's lucky that you should join us, Your Grace," Lady Eastley said once dinner was announced. "With you, we're an even number of couples."

On a normal day, Fitz would flinch at the suggestion of being part of a twosome. But the suggestion of being Lady Wickham's other half – just for the evening – inspired him to grin.

He couldn't have planned to win the wager any more easily. All he had to do was flirt with Lady Wickham – no terrible task – to satisfy Annabelle and Talbot that she was his sweetheart, and then *not* marry her. To not marry a recent widow was perhaps the easiest thing Fitz had ever done.

The dining room was more suited to Edward II's tastes than to modern décor. The stone walls boasted only ancient tapestries and fiery torches, and a bare-bones wooden chandelier illuminated the table. A suit of armor stood at attention next to the sideboard; in the shadows, Fitz mistook it for a footman until the real servant moved.

Yet rather than depress him, Fitz found the medieval setting only boosted his mood. After all, the first duke of Harrodshire had earned the title by defending the crown at home while Richard the Lionheart crusaded in Jerusalem. Fitz had spent many stolen hours of his childhood pretending to be the first duke. How many imaginary maidens had he saved from unsavory rogues, how great had been the mud castles that he defended from French invaders, and how often had his young knees bent in ceremony to receive his knightly title.

Indeed, Bleneccle Manor's dining room inspired the little boy in him to excitement, hoping a ceremony might be right around the corner.

Then again, his excitement might be better traced to Lady Wickham, seated to his right.

"How long have you been visiting Bleneccle Manor?" he asked as the footmen placed plates of roasted quail before them.

"A month or so. We came up for the holidays." As Lady Wickham reached for her crystal goblet of wine, Fitz's eyes were caught by her long, slender fingers, set off nicely with a ruby ring.

He almost didn't notice the plural pronoun she'd used. "We?"

She cut him an amused smile. "My children are

with me, of course. I have two. George, the new Earl of Wickham, and my daughter, Valentina."

Fitz should have guessed, of course, that a young widow would have children. It wasn't as if Wharton had died off in the first year of marriage. Yet he had been so enthralled by Lady Wickham's aura that he hadn't paused to think about the woman living inside it.

He evaluated her now in the hazy light of the chandeliers. Was she in deep grief over the loss of her husband? Was she struggling in the new role of dowager countess, and all the responsibility that came with it? Did she enjoy being a mother?

With the shadows flickering across her eyes, softening her sharp smiles, he couldn't even tell anything as simple as her age. She could have been anywhere from twenty to thirty-five.

Fitz's best route to information was the roundabout route. "How is the new Earl taking to his duties?"

Winpole, seated across the table, let out the delighted, boisterous laugh of a grandfather. "He is four, Your Grace."

Lady Wickham smiled too, though it looked uncomfortable. In a voice almost too low for him to hear, she murmured, "He misses his father, and yet he is barely old enough to understand his father has passed."

Fitz did not consider himself to have much of a heart, so when it constricted in sympathy, he merely thought he was uncomfortable with the sentiment. He didn't remember his own father's death. It had been a mere six months after his birth. Fitz had been the seventh duke for his entire life, and he'd missed his father almost every second.

Lady Wickham watched him with steady, mysterious eyes. Now she shifted in her chair, angling to view him more clearly, as if to redirect the conversation. "How long do you plan to stay with us, Your Grace?"

He appreciated the return to safe territory. "Only as long as it takes for the storm to end and the roads to be safe for carriages again."

Lady Eastley, seated to his left at the head of the table, cut in. "Oh, the roads here are terrible in the winter. If it's not ice, it's snow. If it's not snow, it's mud."

This was not the sort of news Fitz liked to hear. "Talbot's carriage is above average, I'm sure, and can handle ice or mud."

"Ah, but haven't you heard of the northern road toll?"

This from Lady Wickham, her eyes suddenly twinkling in the torch light. Fitz humored her with an amused, "I'm sure my purse can afford it."

She leaned towards him, her voice dropping to let him in on a secret. "The northern road toll is no regular toll, Your Grace. You can't pay in money, nor in fine clothes, nor good horses."

Lady Eastley, on his other side, tittered nervously. "Margot, you do like to poke fun."

Margot. A perfect Christian name if Fitz ever did hear one. He leaned in conspiratorially. "What, must I lay out a glass of wine and a fine roast chicken every night to pay off the spirits?"

Margot – yes, he decided, he could call her by whatever he liked in his thoughts – drew her face into a still, sober mask. "The north doesn't like trespassers, you see. And the roads can tell whether you're a good Northerner or an itinerant Southerner. For us, the mountain passes are wide, smooth, always clear of the snow and mud. But for a Southerner…well, you saw for yourself. Sharp curves no more than a carriage-width deep. Crumbling cliff edges. Snowstorms."

"Lucky for us we have northern friends to take us in."

Margot's eyes gleamed. "For now. But the minute you are back on the road, Your Grace, it will judge you. That's how it decides the toll. If you're a person of good standing, good manners, and goodwill, it may let you go with no more than a broken horseshoe. But if it finds you lacking…you pay a blood price."

"Oh Margot, really!"

But Lady Eastley's shrill exasperation couldn't cut through the spell Margot had cast. Fitz found he couldn't look away from her dark, sparkling eyes, waiting with bated breath for her next words. His heart hammered as fast as if she had put her bare hand on his.

With no more than a ghost tale, she had seduced him.

"And how will I measure up, do you think?" he asked, subconsciously licking his lips, hoping her answer would invite him into the deeper shadows of the castle. She was not the only one who could seduce.

She leaned ever-so-slightly closer. Fitz breathed nothing but her now. If they'd been alone, he would have kissed her. Even now, surrounded by her family, he could barely keep himself from closing the distance. She had the slightest smile on her lips as she spoke, as if she wanted the same.

"Let's see. The Duke of Harrodshire is a man of good standing, indeed. Your manners are, of course, impeccable. What about goodwill? You are traveling to assist your friends with an elopement, which included jilting an innocent young lady on the day of her wedding." In just a few words, Margot's sultry words hardened into ice.

She straightened into the picture of a perfect lady: prim, withdrawn, and emotionless. "Your Grace, you will be found wanting."

Fitz stared. Then he blinked. Then he looked to Lord and Lady Eastley.

Surely he had misheard. Or misunderstood.

Margot had been telling a silly tale. How did it turn into an indictment? And how dare she condemn him, her guest? A duke, to boot?

Could she really hold such a grudge against Talbot and Annabelle?

Lord Eastley had boiled red. "Margot, have you lost your mind?"

The other end of the table silenced. Annabelle was pale, her famed good humor clinging just barely to the corners of her lips.

Margot looked perfectly comfortable. Wearing the fashionable expression of boredom, she murmured, "I do apologize. It was only a joke."

Her eyes didn't even slide to him. That was, perhaps, what most hurt Fitz. That she had enchanted him, only to cast him as an ass. What for him had been the most interesting conversation of his life had, for her, been nothing more than a setup for a set-down.

Fitz could set her down, too. He'd been born for such moments. He could raise an eyebrow in silence. He could cut her with vicious words. He could rebuke the entire party and leave the table.

But he did no such thing. Perhaps because he was still caught in her spell. Perhaps because he simply didn't want any further attention. Perhaps because he agreed: as charming as Annabelle was, Talbot had been wrong to jilt Miss Dawes.

No matter the reason. Fitz raised his glass – which in the dim light appeared full of black ink instead of red wine – in a toast. "That I may learn to laugh, and that you may learn good humor."

Down at the other end of the table, the lady's brother-in-law Osborne chuckled a little too loudly. Winpole chimed in with "hear, hear" a little too quickly. It helped the moment roll by, so no one need dwell on the strange way Lady Wickham had so efficiently cut the duke.

As for the lady herself, Fitz dared not peek. He didn't want to see her reaction, not if it meant watching the enchantress disappear further under a *tonnish* mask. He'd rather finish the evening with civility and retreat to his quiet rooms as soon as it was polite to do so.

Which meant, of course, that he didn't see if his rejoinder had earned a smile of delight, either.

Chapter Four

For the first time in months, Margot was awake in spirit and body all at the same time. She opened her eyes and pushed out of bed in one fell swoop, as if there was a reason for her to be up. As if she was excited to be awake.

She couldn't say just where her energy came from. It had felt good to have company at dinner, even if that company had thrown poor Miss Dawes to the wolves not five days earlier. Margot hadn't expected the mood of the whole house to perk up at the prospect of new faces to please. Even the footmen had seemed to smile more easily as they had set out the banquet.

Margot had to admit she'd enjoyed herself. More than she had in months. There was something to be said for having a goal, even if it was only a goal to make mischief.

There was something to be said, too, for having a duke rake his eyes over one. Especially a handsome duke. Margot had expected someone old and dreary, with a stoop and lazy manners.

The Duke of Harrodshire was anything but that. He stood tall and proud, all long legs and royal cheekbones and curious gray eyes that never seemed restful as they gazed inquisitively through to one's soul.

She had enjoyed being the center of his attention. So

much so that she'd forgotten who he was. That he was aiding and abetting the very marriage that was so hurtful to Miss Dawes. Margot had found herself spinning that story about the northern roads just to keep his eyes on her. It was only when she could feel the heat of his face that she realized what she was doing. Or, rather, realized what she should *not* be doing.

Which was when she'd put her foot in her mouth once and for all.

Margot didn't fully regret her words. They were truthful: the duke *was* found to be wanting, given that he'd condoned his friend's behavior to Miss Dawes. However, she did regret saying them so clearly and loudly and publicly.

Such feelings were much better kept to the drawing room.

Shaking herself from her reverie, Margot decided that no matter where her newfound energy came from, it was best to do what she could to keep it.

Which meant – after dressing and spending half an hour listening to George extoll the virtues of snow – she descended to breakfast in hopes of catching Alice alone. They had to plan their next step.

During the short winter days of January, the Winpole family preferred to eat breakfast in the morning room, where wide glass windows bathed them in sunlight, instead of the dark, stone dining room. Margot was pleased to discover the tradition had been continued even with their guests present, a makeshift banquet table assembled from the side tables and card tables, all draped in a lace cloth.

Unfortunately, Alice was not alone. Not only was Hugh at her side, but their father sat at the head of the table, and none other than the Duke of Harrodshire had taken the seat in the center, a ray of sunshine beaming on his golden hair as he bent over a plate of eggs and sausage.

Margot smoothed her dress, then proceeded to the sideboard, selecting her own portion of soft eggs, bacon, and scones. She took the seat beside Hugh, leaving an empty chair between herself and the duke.

Not that she needed to worry about earning his attention. The duke was engrossed in a conversation with her father, apparently dissecting the responsibilities of counties versus those of the national government.

Alice greeted her with a merry smile. "It's nice to see you up and about so early."

Margot resented the implication – no matter how accurate – that she was not usually at the breakfast table. "I should hate to miss a moment with our guests. Are Lord and Lady Gresham still retired?"

"They already ate. Mother has taken them on a tour of the house."

Margot raised an eyebrow at Alice, hoping her sister understood the silent communication that they needed to speak in private. Then she turned to Hugh. "I'm afraid George has his heart set on an adventure in the snow today. Is there any chance you could take him tromping through the fields? He hates it when I'm the one to accompany him, since I can't be a knight with him."

Dependable Hugh agreed. "It is my honor to bend the knee."

Sensing a lull in the other conversation at the table, Margot turned to the duke. "How do you find Bleneccle Manor in the light of day, Your Grace?"

It was as much a question for herself, to test whether the spell cast at dinner had been an evening bewitchment or if would last into sunshine. She was inclined to call it all a folly, apologize for her behavior, and move forward. But then he set those gray eyes on her again.

"It is a handsome house," he said in a slow, easy drawl. "I confess I was afraid the northern pixies would keep me from sleeping, but I'm well-rested this morning."

He winked with the joke. Margot did not want to admit how it made her stomach trip. Instead, she smiled back. "That would be the blood sacrifice we performed at midnight, to ensure you were protected."

Delight spread across his face, and Margot was sure he was about to laugh when her father intervened. "Never mind Margot, Fitz. She is always finding a new way to torment us. Now, I am most curious to hear about the Warwickshire canal you mentioned. I should like to bring that sort of innovation up here."

Margot didn't consider a joke here and there torment, but she had been receiving such admonishments her whole life, so she barely noticed it until the duke replied. Even as he said "Certainly," to her father, his gray eyes found her again, and he murmured from the corner of his mouth, "I look forward to hearing more about this sacrifice later."

His attention returned to her father; he voiced his opinions on canals even as he turned his shoulders to face Lord Eastley. Yet Margot was aware of the duke with every bite she took. As she poured herself tea, she noted how he held himself tall and proud, his blond hair regal in its old-fashioned queue. As she chatted with Hugh about his new snowplow invention, she heard the bassline of the duke's deep voice. Even when she teased Alice, her thoughts still hooked to whether the duke might overhear.

"If you're quite done eating, may I borrow you for a moment, Margot?" Alice asked, startling Margot from a reverie of what witty tale she might spin next for the duke. Alice raised an amused eyebrow, which Margot chose to ignore.

They retired to Alice's dressing room, ostensibly to choose a brooch for her to wear that evening. Alice chattered on about the importance of cameo details until they were out of earshot of the men, just to keep anyone from asking questions. Then, in the safety of her room, she turned to Margot with a gleam of excitement. "I thought you would never finish eating. I have an idea for what we can do next."

Margot opened Alice's jewelry box and ran her fingers over the set of necklaces shining back up at her. "Do tell."

From a different drawer of her dressing table, Alice withdrew a fat pinecone. "We leave this in Lord Gresham's pillowcase tonight."

It was quite the specimen: both long and broad, it bristled with wide pointers. Margot couldn't help a little laugh. The idea was an infantile prank they might have played on a governess. Yet here they were, grown women.

"What if the maid gets blamed?"

Alice squared her shoulders. "We would intervene, of course. I, for one, don't mind declaring to Lord and Lady Gresham how I feel, if only Mother would allow me."

"Perhaps we should leave a note with the pinecone, for his edification on how to properly treat a young lady." Margot crossed to the window, hoping the morning vista might inspire a better idea. Alice's room looked over the back acres of their property, which sloped upwards until it disappeared into the mountainside. Margot hadn't traveled much before her marriage; it was only once she had taken her honeymoon with Geoff that she'd discovered not all of England was nestled in the soft valleys of friendly mountains. She'd grown accustomed to the flat fields of Wickhamshire, but oh, she was glad to be ensconced in northern fairyland again.

"Well, I'm not sure that insulting the Duke of Harrodshire is a wiser plan," Alice said. "Although I can't say he seems to mind your cheekiness."

The subject was too new for Margot to examine with Alice. Instead, she turned from the mountains and seized the pinecone. "I suppose this is the best we can do, short of mutiny. I feel a little mean about it, but then I remember

Miss Dawes. I suppose she is with her family, and I hope they aren't making her feel too miserable about it."

"Her father wouldn't, but sometimes her mother speaks too stridently." Alice gnawed her lower lip in worry. "What will be worse is the Season. I can't imagine having to return unmarried, when everyone thought you would be on your wedding trip."

What Margot couldn't understand was why Lord Ingram hadn't challenged Lord Gresham instead of letting the man run off with the duchess. Hadn't Lisbeth's father any sense of duty or honor?

It wasn't that Margot approved of duels, but in situations such as these, it would have made Lisbeth's return to the *ton* so much easier had someone stood up for her. Instead, the gossips would whisper about how she'd been deserted by her fiancé and even her father hadn't found her worthy of defense.

It made Margot's blood boil and was enough to make her take up the cause in her own way. Even if it meant sticking a pinecone in a man's pillow.

Her fury matched with the fire leaping in Alice's eyes. "Shall we do this, then?"

Even as daughters of the household, they had no good reason to be in the vicinity of Lord Gresham's bedchamber, so they crept around the castle to avoid discovery by either servant or family. While Alice slipped inside to deposit their present, Margot stationed herself in the hallway, just beyond the door, pretending to examine the portrait of their great-grandfather, the shipping merchant who had earned the barony from Queen Anne. She listened for footsteps, the better to warn Alice, while wishing they had a nobler story to explain their peerage. She'd always longed for a legend of a knight saving a princess from French kidnappers, or a well-fought battle on the Continent, but alas, the Winpoles had been ennobled for richening the royal coffers. The castle they lived in had been a gift at the expense of some Northern lord who dared fight alongside the Scots at the wrong time.

Margot didn't hear any footsteps, but she did hear Alice's shriek. She rushed into the bedchamber to discover Lady Gresham standing in the threshold that adjoined the lord's dressing room, her cool gaze evaluating Alice, whose hand was that very moment stuck inside the pillow.

For a moment, Lady Gresham was still as a statue. She was a tall, slim woman, who could easily have taken up a knight's suit of armor should she need to. Margot wondered if she would be moved to rage, discovering the two of them in her husband's boudoir, and how she would attack. Was she a lady of acerbic wit? Of honey-soaked venom? Or would she let her fury shine through in the privacy of a bedchamber?

The lady stepped forward, a slight smile about her lips. "What a curious scene to walk into. May I ask, Lady Windemere, what you are doing?"

Alice looked to Margot, desperation written across her face. Margot couldn't think of any explanation better than what they were doing – and plenty worse – so she could only give her sister a helpless shrug.

Somehow summoning a haughty expression, Alice withdrew the pinecone and held it aloft for all to see. "Why, I was leaving this in your husband's pillow, Lady Gresham."

Margot and Alice had gotten into a scrape or two as girls, but Margot couldn't recall anything as embarrassing as this. Perhaps because they didn't have the excuse of being children.

Yet Lady Gresham smiled with relief, as if that were what she'd been hoping to hear. "Ah, of course. We're pranking old Talbot. I suppose he deserves it."

The lady sat herself down on the mattress as if they were childhood friends having a chat. "I hope you don't take offense, but as far as pranks go, this one is rather…" here she raised an eyebrow at the pinecone "…rudimentary. Perhaps if we three put our heads together, we can come up with something more sophisticated."

It hardly seemed wise to trust the woman whose husband was the victim, yet something in Lady Gresham's manner made Margot want to. She exchanged a bewildered look with Alice, then took up a seat on the bed as well.

"Now, in matters like this, I like to start with my objective. I assume your objective here is to make Talbot reflect on the consequences his actions will have for Miss Dawes?"

Alice, sitting next to Margot, crossed her arms. "I

would be satisfied with making him hurt in exchange for what he did to Miss Dawes."

"I see." Lady Gresham leaned back, casting her cool blue gaze upwards as she thought. "I have an idea, but we'll need Fitz's help."

Margot thought of the duke's easy, delighted smile at breakfast. She wouldn't mind an excuse to provoke that again.

"We'll have Fitz 'receive a letter' from town with the news that Miss Dawes has published a tell-all article in the scandal sheets about what happened, and that it lists all sorts of falsities. Like that Talbot doesn't know the first thing about horses."

"Or that he doesn't know how to read," Alice suggested.

"That he is afraid to place a bet at White's." Margot earned a little laugh from Lady Gresham before she inquired, "But why does His Grace need to receive the letter? Why couldn't one of us be the recipient?"

"Why, the problem of the unreliable narrator, of course," Lady Gresham responded. "If you're the one reading the letter, Talbot will have an inkling that perhaps you are exaggerating. Whereas he trusts his best friend. He won't conceive that Fitz is in on the joke."

Alice was gnawing her lower lip again. "If they're best friends, will His Grace agree to participate?"

Lady Gresham's face lit with mischief. "I believe he will if Lady Wickham asks him."

Margot felt her face heat with a blush as both women

turned the same amused smile on her. "Me? I only met the man last night. Why should he do anything I ask him to?"

"If he gives you any trouble, just bat your eyes at him a few times like you did at dinner last night," Lady Gresham said. "I believe he's partial to it."

As her sister hid a giggle, Margot stood, the better to maintain her dignity. "I was only batting my eyes last night to teach His Grace a lesson on leaving poor, innocent debutantes with their honor impugned on their wedding day. I shall gladly do so again with the same mission."

"And I shall work on the letter," Alice declared. "Perhaps we can have it 'arrive' by special messenger this evening."

"It's a plan." Lady Gresham headed back to the interior door that led to Talbot's dressing room. She paused at the threshold. "In the meantime, I'll brace for whatever variation of the pinecone you have planned for me. After all, it was I who proposed to Talbot, knowing he was to be married the next morning. Although, in the end, I believe it was Miss Dawes who convinced him to run off with me."

The words hung in the air even after Lady Gresham shut the door behind her. Margot turned to Alice, who looked a little queasy. "It doesn't matter whose idea it was," Margot reminded her. "Miss Dawes is the one who suffers, and Lord Gresham is the one who got his heart's desire."

Alice nodded.

"Our goal is to make sure he knows *we* know that Miss Dawes deserved better."

Alice nodded again. Then she turned a smile on Margot. "I'm beginning to regret our wager. If you keep up these spirits, you'll have no trouble winning, and then I'll end up with a firstborn named Bartholomew."

"I am leaning towards Vladimir, actually." Margot took her hand. "Let's get out of this bedroom before we're caught again, and you have to explain it to your husband."

"Or you have to explain it to your duke," Alice shot back.

"He's hardly *my* duke, and I'll thank you to remember that."

Yet Margot had to admit – to herself, and no one else – that she was thrilled by the idea that her eyelashes had any effect on him at all.

Chapter Five

Ensconced in his little private sitting room, Fitz supposed things had worked out in his favor, all things considered. True, their journey was delayed at least another night while they waited for the snows to melt from the road; and also true, Fitz itched to return to Pembroke Abbey before reporting to London for the February sessions. Yet, being trapped in Bleneccle Manor really wasn't the worst of fates.

For one thing, he and Winpole had a very productive discussion at breakfast regarding the apothecary initiative. Winpole had broad, loud opinions, very much in keeping with his general person, and on the whole, they tended to the conservative side of progress. However, he was Fitz's favorite kind of conservative: one willing to compromise. If Fitz supported his private bill to build a canal connecting Bleneccle Manor to the Irish Sea, then Winpole was more than happy to vote in favor of Fitz's 'pet' apothecary bill.

There was nothing that put Fitz in a good mood such as striking a deal, particularly in the name of moving the realm forward.

Another point in favor of their northern detour was the very sitting room he now occupied. Though small – it would barely fit four people for socializing – the room was cozy and well-appointed, with a generous hearth. Long, wide windows admitted plenty of pale winter sun, with comfortable leather chairs inviting one to open a book for the afternoon.

A knock at the door reminded Fitz of the final point in favor of his wintry prison. None other than Margot stood at the other side, a slightly mischievous smile wreathing her lips. He had discovered at breakfast that, in daylight, Margot's dark hair gleamed with a few threads of gold, and her eyes danced with honey. Her cheeks warmed with delicious blushes, too, which he hadn't been able to see by candlelight.

He wasn't usually one to enjoy eliciting blushes from a lady, but it would be good fun with Margot.

Shaking himself of such thoughts, Fitz greeted Margot with a slight bow.

"I'm sorry for disturbing your privacy, Your Grace," she said, her voice a rush of breathless words. "I wondered if I might borrow a book from this library."

Stepping back to let her in, Fitz couldn't help but wonder how desperately she really wanted a specific book. His blood quickened at the hope that perhaps she had conjured up the need as an excuse.

An excuse to enter his private chambers.

"I thought I asked you to call me Fitz," he said.

A lovely blush crept behind her ears. "I supposed I had lost that privilege last night."

He leaned against the stone threshold. There was something lovely in the idea that she had sat up feeling guilty for her words. "I'm not so sensitive that I would hold a little fairy story against you. Though I daresay you insulted Lord and Lady Gresham."

Fury flashed across her whole body – from the clench of her eyebrows down to her feet stepping into fighting stance – as quick and as brief as lightning. "That was rather the point," she said, before softening again, a regretful smile at her lips.

She still stood just inside the room, a mere arm's distance from Fitz, and he wondered again what really brought her visiting. It was his good fortune that she was there. She was the perfect dalliance, a sweetheart who could never be his wife. Besides the fact that she was a widow and guardian to an earl, Fitz needed a duchess who would stand calmly at his side, unflinching as they managed the *ton*, foreign diplomats, and his tenants alike.

A woman ruled by emotion such as Margot was best kept as a friend, not a wife.

Fitz decided to test how committed she was to her excuse. "Were you here for a specific book, or did you hope to browse?"

There came that lovely blush again, reaching just to the tips of her ears. "A specific book. I'd had it in my room until a few days ago, but I suppose a well-meaning maid put it away."

She crossed to the shelves just below the lead-paned windows and knelt to slide a thick cloth-and-board book from its spot. Fitz watched with a mixture of disappointment and fascination as Margot caressed the spine, then held the book to her nose, inhaling its scent the way young brides inhaled their bouquets.

Fitz resisted the urge to close the distance between them. The room was small enough that even from the other side of it, he could smell her rose water perfume. Still, he prodded, "It must be a very dear book to you."

Margot beamed. "*Paradise Lost*. It is my best friend when I'm in the depths of despair. Shakespeare's sonnets are just the thing when I'm in a good mood, but when I am sad, there is no comfort but Milton. I need his strange combination of faith and wickedness to sustain me. And I always comfort myself knowing at least I haven't gone blind yet."

Clutching the book to her breast, she did not look much like a woman in despair. Yet Fitz supposed that was the thing about grief; one never could count on being free of it.

"*Paradise Lost* was my favorite in school, though I've never been partial to verse myself," Fitz admitted. "I prefer histories, if I'm doing leisure reading."

"The only use I have for histories is to put me to sleep." Margot said this with a certain friendly spark of challenge in her eye. "Unless it is about knights of yore. My son George and I share a fondness for anything to do with knights in armor."

"Must they be Knights of the Round Table, or do you care for the real knights of the Crusades, as well?"

"Any knight will do, as long as they are in shining armor, for George's sake, and have a maiden waiting for them at home, for mine."

Fitz had noted a copy of *Lancelot, the Knight of the Cart* tucked beside a history of the Roman Empire. Now he retrieved it from the shelf. "Have you read this one with little Wharton yet? It was my favorite poem as a boy."

Margot took the little volume with care, tucking it on top of her *Paradise Lost.* "I read it years ago, but I haven't shared it with George yet. It's quite scandalous, isn't it, with Lancelot stealing Queen Guinevere from King Arthur?"

Fitz had never much fixated on the romance of it. What he remembered were Lancelot's numerous battles on his way to Guinevere, the jousts, and the agony of a knight lowering himself to be carried in a cart. It had been a lesson in what a man must be willing to do to carry on his quest; he hadn't paid a whit of attention to the adultery.

"I don't suppose Guinevere owed King Arthur much loyalty after he let her be kidnapped," he responded. "A wife's loyalty should only extend as far as her husband's, and King Arthur surely wasn't being loyal when he walked into Meleagant's trap."

Margot's eyebrows spiked in amusement. "I believe the Bible says otherwise, but I suppose a bachelor such as yourself hasn't had to pay attention to such details before."

She was right; though suddenly, Fitz was captivated, wondering how often she had contemplated adultery as a married woman and whether it had been on her behalf or old Wharton's. Or both.

"I was going to sit down with a book," Fitz said, gesturing to the chairs. "I'd welcome the company, if you would care to join me."

Margot followed the direction of his hand with a dubious glance. To sit alone with him in the room adjoining his bedchamber – even if only reading – would certainly invite speculation, should anyone see them. Fitz had offered it in part to test just how much she had really wanted that copy of *Paradise Lost*, but truly, he wouldn't mind spending the afternoon with her. He suspected there were many debates they could get into.

"I can't stay, for I promised to help Alice," Margot said at last, rushing out the words like a debutante fishing for an acceptable excuse.

Fitz allowed himself to feel a little dip of disappointment. "Ah, I imagine sisters can be quite demanding."

This earned a smile, the kind she'd bestowed on him last night while spinning her tale. "You cannot begin to know. Speaking of which, I wonder if you would help us with a little lark this evening."

"I am at your service."

"You see, as special friends of Miss Dawes, Alice and I would like to show Lord Gresham what we think of his behavior. We have solicited Lady Gresham's support – so as not to cause irreparable offense – and she suggested a plan that depends upon none other than you."

So she did have an ulterior motive for her visit. Fitz was glad to know he'd been right, though he wished the motive had been more related to his charm. "Lady Gresham supports this?"

"It was her idea." Margot's eyes flashed again, but instead of anger, Fitz picked up on a touch of admiration. "We're going to deliver a letter that claims Miss Dawes is publishing her account of the episode in the Times. We'll include all sorts of dreadful falsehoods – Lady Gresham suggested we claim that Lord Gresham knows nothing about horses – and make him feel really awful and nervous about it. Alice is writing the letter, but we need you to be the one to receive it and read it, so that Lord Gresham won't suspect it is a sham"

Fitz could just imagine Talbot quaking in his seat at such a letter. His friend felt badly enough about the whole situation; the man didn't need any further torment. But if Annabelle was in on the joke, then it must not be too bad.

Still, Fitz felt that as the man's best friend, he must at least attempt to stop the prank. "Miss Dawes really was much happier not to get married that morning, you know. I was there. I daresay I've never seen a more blissful bride, once they announced it was off."

The friendliness that had softened Margot throughout their whole interview disappeared, and she regarded him with a brittle, fiery distance. "This is about the principle of the thing. Frankly, the men in the Dawes family should be defending Miss Dawes's honor, but since they are letting her name be dragged through the mud, we must stand up for her instead."

Hostility was a natural progression of negotiation. Fitz dealt with it a hundred times throughout each Parliamentary season. Still, there was something about Margot's anger that made Fitz's heart race in fear that he had lost her goodwill altogether. He opened his palms in peace. "I have every intention of dancing the first set with Miss Dawes when she returns to town. That should set her up with enough suitors to have a dozen offers by the end of the Season."

"How kind of you," Margot said. "Will you read the letter this evening, too?"

Fitz reviewed the woman in front him. Swathed in gray widow's weeds, clutching books to her chest, standing straight and erect, she shouldn't have been beautiful. She should have made him think of his severe governesses or the fussy matrons who guarded society too jealously. She stared at him with a steady power that surely she used on her children, intense and heavy with the expectation that he would do as she bid.

Fitz shouldn't have felt a surge of admiration, yet he did.

And he shouldn't have wanted to kiss her, but he yearned for it, as he'd never yearned to kiss any woman before.

He reined it in, of course. He hoped his eyes were cool, his expression clear of any of those strange thoughts, as he answered. "For you, my lady, I will."

Margot's lips curved in victory. "Then we shall look forward to the evening post." She floated out the door, pausing in the threshold – so close to him again – long enough to throw him one last look over her shoulder. "Thank you, too, for the book recommendation."

Fitz nodded helplessly, watching her sashay down the corridor. He wondered if this was how his Parliament friends felt when he bargained them into his corner. Like they didn't quite know what had just happened. Like their thoughts had been whipped into a new shape they'd never seen before.

Like his heart might never be the same.

Chapter Six

Evenings came early to Bleneccle Manor in the winter. Dusk fell as soon as half past three, before they had even given George and Valentina an afternoon snack of bread and butter. It was Margot's personal theory that her family was so lively precisely because of these yawning dark winter hours. One *had* to be entertaining, or else end up like poor Hugh before he married Alice, sitting in silence across the hearth from his mother.

Still, this winter, the evenings had been especially dreary. Even that day, with all the excitement of the morning, something dark and deep settled on Margot's heart as the sun went down. She was accustomed to slow days with George's boyish exploits forming the only excitement; the episodes with Lady Gresham and the duke – Fitz, he'd reminded her, and how secretly delicious it was to call him that in her thoughts – left her head spinning. Instead of dressing for the evening, Margot was tempted to climb into bed, burrow under her blankets, and pretend the world had stopped turning.

Alas, there were children to tend to and guests to entertain.

George and Valentina quizzed her on what the adults would get up to as she kissed them goodnight in the nursery, where they would have their supper and be allowed to play until seven. Would they collect costumes for charades? Would Aunt Alice play the harpsichord for singing? Would they stay up all night playing cards? Valentina went so far as to suggest that Margot don her ballgown, for there were surely enough gentlemen for a dance.

Their excitement only increased when Alice swept into the nursery dressed in her dinner gown. It was one of her finer dresses, trimmed with lace about the neck and sleeves, and she'd added a string of pearls at her neck for ornamentation. Valentina grabbed at her skirts in awe, begging Aunt Alice to please give her doll a kiss.

Alice complied, then straightened with a fierce glitter of anger. "I'm not speaking to Hugh," she informed Margot.

"Oh?" Margot took in the flush of her sister's face, the heat in her voice, and decided the best response was teasing. "Are we back to the theory that he plotted to ruin you?"

Alice scoffed. "He told me I must set aside our plans and try to be nice to Lord and Lady Gresham. He actually used the word 'must'!"

Margot hadn't thought Hugh had the backbone to give Alice advice, much less try to order her around. She imagined he hadn't been quite as firm as Alice heard him. "I'm sure he meant it as a suggestion."

"Lord Gresham had a private word with him after luncheon to confide that Lady Gresham was feeling unwelcome. Now Hugh thinks I'm being uncharitable and mean. He doesn't think Lisbeth would want me to behave this way. Can you imagine it? After we took Lady Gresham into our confidence, too."

"Lady Gresham probably didn't share with her husband that we are now chums, given our plans," Margot countered. "Besides, we *are* being uncharitable and mean." She remembered the way Fitz had tried to evade the favor. The way he had squirmed mixed a strange combination of guilt and tenderness in her heart, which she preferred to cover with a steady flame of anger. "We must be, since that is our only recourse once men fail us."

"Indeed. I daresay you don't miss Geoff *today*," Alice huffed. She thundered on before Margot could quite process the comment, much less respond. "Besides, we're not being mean to *Lady* Gresham. Even if she does claim that she proposed to him, Lord Gresham was the one with the obligation to Lisbeth."

"And once we've taught him his lesson with the letter, we'll set the matter aside," Margot reminded her. "Fitz has promised to dance Lisbeth's first set this Season, which should set her up with dozens of suitors."

Alice's eyebrows shot up to her hairline. "*Fitz* has, has he? Did he say so with a charming smile, too?"

Margot pulled a face at her sister. "We had better get downstairs, don't you think?"

"I'd rather hear more about your conversation with *Fitz*. What else did he promise?"

Nurse entered with the children's supper, saving Margot from this line of questioning. A seasoned Wickhamshire woman, she'd been with Margot since

George's birth, and felt familiar enough to exclaim, "Shouldn't my ladies be downstairs? I daresay everyone else is in the drawing room."

"Quite right, Nurse." Margot looped her arm through Alice's. "I believe something interesting came by messenger, too."

"Yes, yes, but remember, I'm not speaking to Hugh."

Margot didn't think *that* would last long. Alice and Hugh were too smitten to do anything but send each other moon eyes across the room when they were forced to separate. But in the name of sisterly solidarity, she promised to remember.

The atmosphere of the drawing room was considerably more relaxed than it had been the previous evening. Even their mother had let down her guard, laughing with Lady Gresham rather than keeping a watchful eye to make sure everyone was enjoying themselves. The only two who seemed uncomfortable were Hugh – who kept glancing over at Alice, as if hoping she might suddenly forgive him – and Fitz, who stood stiffly by the mantel, sipping his sherry with a distinct look of distraction while her father droned at him about the canal project.

Margot was tempted to interrupt – she even knew what little sly joke she would make to put a smile on Fitz's lips – but she so hated any conversation about improvement, and her father was more likely to dismiss her than to let her break up his soliloquy on why Fitz should invest in canals.

It was just as Geoff had been with his cotton mill. The mill wasn't the first project that replaced Margot as the object of Geoff's fascination, but it had lasted the longest. He had spent so much time on that mill – researching it, talking about it, overseeing its construction, checking in on its operations – that Margot hardly saw him, and when she did, it was all he spoke about. She was more jealous of the mill than of any love affair he could have had.

Margot decided to be charitable and sit with Hugh, instead, who was beginning to look quite miserable. "Fear not," she murmured. "You know she just needs to get it out of her system, like Valentina when she hasn't had her nap."

Hugh responded with a little helpless shrug. "I know it, and yet..."

"And yet you love her." A snake of envy slithered across Margot's stomach. She dismissed it; no matter that Geoff's love for her hadn't lasted past their honeymoon. She'd had a nice friendship with her husband, which was more than many wives could say, and if his worst crime had been to spend too much time on a mill, she supposed she didn't have much to gripe about.

She absolutely refused to turn bitter simply because her sister had better luck.

Margot was glad of the distraction when Fitz finally broke away from her father. Moving beside Lord Gresham's seat on the settee – where they could all hear him plain as day – he cleared his throat. "I had an interesting letter from my man in town today. He wrote with news of Miss

Dawes."

Beside her, Hugh groaned. Meanwhile, Alice perked up, all innocence as she asked eagerly, "Oh? Good news, I hope? I do worry about her so."

Lord Gresham's face already matched his red hair in hue.

Fitz's gray eyes flicked to Margot, as if asking one last time whether this was really what she meant him to do. She met him with what she hoped was a look of encouragement.

Fitz unfolded the letter. "Miss Dawes means to publish an account of…the affair…in the *Times*." He paused, glancing at Lord Gresham, who was doing his best not to grimace.

Good, Margot thought. *He deserves it.*

From the other side of the room, Lady Gresham said, "Of course she has every right. Do you have any details?"

"My man managed to get the copy she submitted to the editors. I'm afraid it contains all sorts of claims, including that you cried off at the altar, not before the ceremony began; that as much as you talk about race horses, you get every fact wrong; that your secretary must read every correspondence aloud to you because you are yourself illiterate; and that Ambley Park is close to bankruptcy, so you and whichever Lady Gresham is attached to you will need to flee to France to outrun your creditors."

Margot hadn't read the final letter that Alice had submitted and gasped a little at the last claim. Her father bellowed, "For shame! I didn't think Miss Dawes capable of such a thing."

Lord Gresham was still as a rock and red as a lobster. "I didn't expect it, but I deserve it, of course. She wished us the best, but after a few days, she would feel differently. I'm only glad she limited her attacks to myself and didn't say anything about Lady Gresham."

"It's nothing but slander!" Lord Eastley insisted. "If I were you, I would call her father out to settle this score. She can't go publishing such rubbish in the papers without consequence."

Margot had seen her father angry before – it was from him that she had learned to bluster from bliss to fury in a matter of seconds – but never had he spoken one word in encouragement of duels. His opinion had always been that they were illegal, old-fashioned, and in poor taste. She stared at him in disbelief. "She can publish whatever she likes. Lord Gresham has ruined her reputation; why shouldn't she retaliate?"

"He's hardly *ruined* her reputation," Lord Eastley shot back. "She is still a genteel lady of good standing. If she publishes this, then her reputation will be ruined, that's for sure. Who would want to marry a woman that spiteful?"

"You're right. This will ruin her." This from Lord Gresham, whose face was now as pale as the snow outside. For a moment, he stared at nothing. Then he popped from his seat. "I shall write my own account to the *Times*, verifying everything Miss Dawes claims. It may hurt our reputation, but it will save her from her own folly."

He was a scraggly man with hair too red, and he wore only a fine evening suit, yet for a moment, Margot could see him as an armored knight, off to protect the wronged woman.

Even though he was the one who had wronged her.

Margot turned her attention to Alice, putting all her energy in silently urging her sister to give up the act. She hardly needed to try; Alice beamed at Lord Gresham.

"Oh, I see now your heart is so good, my lord! Would you mind terribly if I broke all rules of propriety and gave you a hug?" Alice didn't wait for an answer – neither from poor Lord Gresham nor her husband nor Lady Gresham – but threw her arms around the man's neck. "You see, Miss Dawes is my best friend, so I had to avenge her in some way. Never did I imagine you would throw yourself on the sword in her name."

Free of her embrace, Lord Gresham looked merely bewildered. "I don't understand. You wrote the account in the *Times*?"

"There is no account in the *Times*!"

"Oh Alice," Lady Eastley sighed.

Fitz handed Lord Gresham the letter while Alice explained. "I wrote the letter and handed it to His Grace this afternoon. It's all made up, you see. We wanted to make you suffer, as poor Miss Dawes has. Now that you have proven how noble you are, we may put all this behind us and be friends again."

"We?" Lord Gresham echoed.

"I'm afraid it was a group effort," Fitz said, slapping a hand against his friend's arm. "Even Annabelle helped us out."

Lady Gresham came to stand next to her husband now with a mischievous smile. "The part about running off to France was my idea."

Margot stood, too, if only to confess to her part in the scheme. "Do you think you'll recover, Lord Gresham?"

He looked from one to the other for a long moment, and Margot feared perhaps they had really crossed a line.

Then Lord Gresham laughed. He shook Fitz's hand, dotted little bows to Alice and Margot, and finally pressed a kiss to his wife's hand. "It's like when schoolboys knock their friends down, I suppose. Now we can call ourselves even."

"Exactly!" Alice exclaimed. "Lord Windemere tried to stop me from doing it, but you see, now the whole atmosphere will be festive."

"It already *was* festive," their mother said from her corner. "I, for one, protest your actions, but as all's well that ends well, that will be the sum of what I say on the subject."

Lord Eastley, for his part, was glowering at the whole group, as if he couldn't quite figure out what had happened. Finally, he shook his head. "Lord Gresham, if I may give you a piece of advice? Never have daughters."

The group laughed at this, and her father poured

everyone another round of sherry, yet Margot couldn't quite smile along. The letter had done its job; they had avenged Miss Dawes, and she truly believed Lord Gresham had only the best intentions in his heart. But where Margot had expected anger from Lord Gresham, she hadn't anticipated the fury from her father. She might have predicted he would dismiss the letter as silly; she never would have guessed he would respond with such violent anger.

Why it should bother her so, Margot couldn't say; yet she couldn't shake the sensation that something was wrong with her father's reaction.

Alice interrupted Margot's ruminating. "Margot, could you please request that my husband put that book away and join the conversation?"

Lost in her own thoughts, Margot hadn't noticed that Hugh had started scribbling in a little notebook. Now he straightened, grimaced guiltily, and slipped the pad and pencil back into his pocket. Margot said, "Apparently, your wife still isn't speaking to you."

Hugh tried, "I would be happy to join the conversation, Lady Windemere."

"Margot, please inform my husband I meant he should speak to someone *other* than me."

Margot turned to Lady Gresham, who was observing it all with an amused smile. "Lady Gresham, would you be so kind as to inform my sister that she should handle her own communications?"

Alice's eyes flashed with humor at this. Lady Gresham

carried the game forward with, "Lord Windemere, would you be a dear and inform your wife that her sister is no longer willing to be her communications conduit?"

This was enough to make Alice laugh, and Hugh joined in happily. Lady Gresham turned to Margot. "Lady Wickham, if I may, you're looking a little piqued. Fitz, why don't you take her for a little walk to escape the crowd of this room?"

Margot was alarmed at the observation; she had just been smiling at Hugh, after all. Yet she couldn't object. For one, she *was* feeling piqued and wouldn't mind an escape from all the polite banter. For another, Fitz had already risen, his friendly eyes resting on her.

"I haven't yet seen Bleneccle Manor's gallery," he said. "Perhaps you would be so good as to show me?"

He didn't offer his arm, and Margot didn't take it. They kept so appropriate a distance from each other that no matron of Almack's London ballroom would whisper. Yet Margot could feel him beside her during the whole walk from the drawing room to the back of the castle, where their finer artwork hung on display.

"Papa hasn't yet added on a modern wing of the house, so our gallery is rather makeshift, I'm afraid," Margot apologized. "This was originally the great room where the lord presided over his feasts."

Now the room was large and empty, save for the artwork on the walls. Most of the paintings were family portraits, accumulated through the years, though the section nearest the door featured French paintings her father had acquired on his trips to London throughout her childhood. The servants, not anticipating any visitors to the gallery, had lit only the wall sconces, scattering dark webs of shadows through the hall.

It was horribly romantic, the perfect place for a secret tryst.

Not that Margot expected Fitz harbored any romantic intentions towards her. Not that she wanted him to.

As if rebuking her thoughts, Fitz dutifully turned to consider the painting beside the door, an interpretation of Samson and Delilah. "Do you miss living in this castle when you return south?" he asked. "I daresay it is quite different from…what is the name of your country home?"

"Corinium Park." Whenever she pictured her house, it was as she'd first seen it in her marital carriage. She had squeezed Geoff's hand in excitement until he'd cried off in pain. Their house rose from the center of a demure, green parkland, a white stone monument that sparkled when the sun decided to shine. Unlike the circular staircases and crenellations of Bleneccle Manor, Corinium Park was all stately lines and rectangular windows surveying open space.

Now she felt a pang of homesickness. Her little dominion of Wickhamshire was bustling and grand compared to the quiet winters of Bleneccle Manor. How she loved to spend an afternoon in the village, delivering food to the cottages and visiting with the tradesmen.

Margot realized she missed it.

"Corinium Park is very different," she answered Fitz. "I loved this castle growing up. It has so many nooks and crannies for mischief."

He moved along to the next painting. "Will you have to return to Corinium Park soon?"

Ah, the question most likely to plunge her into gloom. Yet, at least for that moment, Margot almost wished she were already there. Oh, she could do without Mrs. Preston's brusque household updates and Mr. Robbins's demands about the estate, but to visit with her tenants and hear their good country sense – that would be a treat.

"I suppose so. We've been gone since November. Of course, my steward hardly needs me to keep things running, but I did miss showering everyone with their Christmas gifts."

Fitz gave her a rather queer look at this, as if he didn't quite know what to make of it.

Oh, how Margot wished she could straighten herself out, so she didn't say odd things like this in the middle of a perfectly nice conversation. She changed the subject. "Lord Gresham took the letter in stride, don't you think?"

"I knew he would." There was a touch of obstinate loyalty in Fitz's tone that warmed Margot. Then those gray eyes settled on her again. "Do you feel better, having exacted your revenge?"

Had her father uttered the words, Margot's hackles would have gone up in defense. Indeed, her first reaction was to bristle, before she realized Fitz wasn't belittling her; he was simply asking how she felt.

And she realized she felt defensive because now that the excitement of the letter was over, her spirits were just as low as ever.

"I'm glad to know Lord Gresham isn't resting on his laurels," she said carefully. She didn't want to get into the murky state of her emotions with Fitz. He was friendly and handsome and witty, but none of that meant he wanted to hear about the strange murmurings of her heart. Yet somehow, Margot's mouth prattled on without her. "Alice drummed it all up, to lift my spirits, you know. I suppose she thought some mischief would be enough to return me to my old self."

The words out in the air, Margot resisted the urge to clap a hand over her mouth in horror. She risked a glance at Fitz, who had turned from the paintings to regard her fully. He really was so tall, yet no part of his presence was threatening. Even as he listened to an addled widow confess to ugly emotions.

"Whenever I have been low," he said slowly, "I've had friends with similar inclinations. A gentleman can get up to all sorts of mischief. Yet no amount of ale or gambling or boxing has ever shaken me of low spirits. For me, the only trick is to set myself a goal, and then to work hard to achieve it."

Margot's thoughts trailed on the image of Fitz in some pub. She couldn't picture it. He was too composed, always prepared with the perfect polite response, to descend into hell dens.

"I don't mean to preach morals, though it may sound that way," he continued. "It's just that achieving something is so much more powerful than sulking. And mischief, in the end, is only an active form of sulking."

Catching up to the content of his advice, Margot turned the idea over in her head. It was fine and dandy for a duke to set goals. He had a seat in the House of Lords and dozens of entailments.

She was a mere lady. She had children to raise, to be sure, but beyond that, Margot was largely a symbol. Symbols didn't need goals.

Yet as soon as she dismissed the idea, it rebounded back. Why shouldn't she have goals? Why shouldn't she do as much as Geoff had, if not more?

So what if most people saw her simply as a statuette of good breeding. Margot could seize that and use it to her advantage.

All she needed was a vision for what she wanted to accomplish.

Chapter Seven

Fitz wished he could take back the last five minutes. His thoughts – so earnest in his head – had tumbled out into the world sounding as pompous as could be, and now Margot was staring at him with wide, blank eyes as if he were the biggest idiot in the world.

No, her eyes weren't quite blank. There was a spark to her expression that hinted at a million thoughts rushing behind them, but she chose not to say any of them. Which meant they were all unkind. At his expense. And well they should be. Had he really just spouted to her the virtues of *setting a goal?*

Fitz's mind raced for a way to fix this. Margot was too lovely to be subjected to his bumbling. He would spoil their friendship if he carried on like this.

Oh, he was adept at catering to overdeveloped egos or wasting hours listening to a man unburden his soul. He knew how to read a room and how to play the cards dealt by whomever he needed in his corner; it was the natural talent that made him so effective as the Diplomatic Duke.

But add emotions – real, raw feelings, especially those of a woman – into the mix, and he was at a loss.

Fitz had been brought up to believe emotions were mere excuses invoked by the weak to slip out of their duties. His mother certainly had never let him show any tears, nor laughter. He'd learned over the years that not everyone took this view. The first time a woman had cried before him – Loretta Billings, a young lady dancing with him at a house party – he'd advised her to tuck away her tears before she embarrassed herself, and she'd slapped him. By the time he was twenty-two and had installed the actress Sylvie Stanton as his mistress, he'd learned to be less callous, yet when Sylvie cried to him over her father's death, he'd only managed to make her angry, not cheer her up.

Now here was Margot, not even close to tears, and Fitz quaked. She had not revealed much of her heart – in fact, Fitz suspected from a little flame in her eyes that she regretted saying as much as she had. Still, in what she did say, Fitz could feel her soul churning with something more than he could identify. And even though he knew he couldn't console her, he was overcome with a desperate need to do so.

Hence, his deaf suggestion that she *set a goal*.

The woman before him had already mothered two children. She didn't need a lecture on managing one's life. She needed empathy.

Margot still stood there, staring at his idiocy. The torchlight sparkled off her hair and eyes, making even her gray gown seem golden. Of course, in the moment when he should be finding something better to say, he would be distracted by her beauty. He knew better than to comment on it; Margot wasn't the kind of vain woman who would be cheered out of grief by a sonnet on the perfect pink curve of her lips, though they were rosy and slender, and he imagined wonderful to kiss.

"Perhaps it should be a goal you wouldn't normally attempt," he found himself saying, as if expounding on the topic would make it better. "Something you wouldn't normally dare to do."

Margot blinked a few times, treating Fitz to a lovely show of dark, seductive lashes. "I rather think that was Alice's intention with the prank on Lord Gresham."

At least she hadn't slapped him yet. "Perhaps something bigger. With a little more meaning. Wharton built a cotton mill, did he not? Perhaps you want to build a railway to connect the mill to the port."

Now she frowned, her eyebrows spiking in fury. Fitz supposed his good luck was running out on him. And they still had a whole dinner to sit through together.

But Margot only said, "I don't know the first thing about building a railway."

So glad was he at this answer, that he dared a smile. "I daresay Wharton didn't know the first thing about cotton mills until he decided to build one. None of us do. We hire men to tell us what we need to know."

"But I'm a woman."

"I'd noticed." He couldn't help himself from giving that response, nor from dipping his eyes down her body at the very mention of the word. Somehow, one or the other of them had stepped forward, and they were rather inappropriately close to each other. "You're a dowager countess with wealth and power. I don't see why you shouldn't be able to build a railroad if you want to."

"I hate Geoff's cotton mill."

"Then don't build a railroad. Do whatever you want."

Their voices had dropped to soft murmurs. When he inhaled, Fitz breathed in the scent of Margot's rose water and powder. His fingers tingled with the urge to take her hands in his.

"I don't know what I want," Margot whispered. Her eyes darted down to his lips – he could have sworn they did. He wondered if she was losing track of her thoughts, too.

"I envy you. It is so much fun to discover what one wants." He sought her gaze again, those beautiful honeyed irises that lived with such intensity. "For example, I've just discovered that I want to kiss you, and I'm filled with a thrill."

She blushed. He could see it, even in the torchlight, a crimson that reached all the way to the tip of her nose. At the same time, that lovely wicked mischief snuck back into her eyes. "It's the northern pixies playing a trick on you. If you kiss me, you'll be trapped here all winter."

Fitz inched closer. "I'm willing to pay the price. If you'd like me to, that is. What do you say?"

"Oh," she breathed, "I want you to kiss me."

She might have been a pixie herself, the way her eyes glowed gold as Fitz leaned down. He kissed her gently at first, relishing her perfect lips, then again more ardently when her fingers flew around his neck. Her very touch set every nerve on fire. Fitz felt so light and airy, he would have believed fairy dust had set them flying about the picture gallery. When finally he drew away with a ragged breath, Margot glistened with an unbridled smile.

"Well," she said.

"Well," he echoed. Their foreheads still rested against each other, for he couldn't bear to part with her entirely just yet.

"I suppose we should return to the group," Margot murmured. Indeed, Fitz now tuned into laughter from the front of the castle, and the enticing smell of roast turkey drifted through the air.

How Annabelle would gloat, now that they'd spent so long alone in the gallery. Even if they could suppress the magic of the kiss from their demeanors – which Fitz wasn't sure he could – she would wink at him and suppose they were sweethearts.

Well, he didn't mind that. Margot as his special someone was certainly a nice adventure. Annabelle could gloat all she wanted. He still had control over whom he would marry. Pixie that she was, Margot would dance out of his life as quickly as she'd floated into it.

He would mourn it, to be sure, but he would win the wager.

Chapter Eight

Margot was still spinning the next day, even as she sat next to her mother in the morning room with a cushion to embroider. Lady Gresham – who had begun insisting they all call her Annabelle, on account of how familiar they were since the little prank – perched on the old stiff-backed walnut chair that, as a girl, Margot had pretended was a throne; Alice completed the group on the low-slung upholstered chair a cousin had once brought as a gift. It was a room full of conversationalists, and so her companions gabbed away, here catching Annabelle up on gossip, there parsing the futility of such-and-such a law. On a normal day, Margot would relish it, so far from the dull murmurs of the average London drawing room.

Not that morning. She had too much to turn over in her own head to enjoy the chatter around her.

If she closed her eyes, Margot could still recall the soft fire of Fitz's kiss. Her fingers remembered the delicious scratch of his shaven cheek. His hand – for just a moment – had found the curve of her waist, and she could feel it there still, warm and urgent.

All this, if she dared remember it. Margot had spent the entirety of dinner and most of the night desperately trying *not* to. Surely it was wicked to be kissing a man not even a year after Geoff had died. No matter that one day she hated Geoff and the next she missed him; she was his widow, still wearing her weeds. She had no business paying favors to any other man.

But as soon as she finished scolding herself, Fitz's face would pop back into her mind's eye. It wasn't the vision of him after the kiss – smoky eyes and a smile lazy upon his lips – but rather the look he'd given her when he'd said, "Build a railroad." As if it were obvious. And simple. And the natural thing to do when one was blue.

Never mind that Margot had never considered she could now play Geoff's part. None other than a duke thought she *should*.

That tumbled her thoughts in a whole new direction. She knew she didn't care for a railroad, but what did she want? And how could she possibly find out? She couldn't possibly learn by trial and error on projects so large. She had to discover her own mind.

Margot had never doubted that she knew her own mind until Geoff died. Now, apparently, she was the type of woman who insulted house guests and threw herself at dukes.

Which brought her back to that kiss.

Margot was sighing anew, remembering how her whole body had responded to Fitz's confession that he'd wanted to kiss her, when she noticed a pause in the conversation around her. Snapping back into the present, she followed her companions' gazes out of the great big windows of the morning room to see a man on horseback coming down the drive.

"Who on earth could it be?" her mother wondered aloud, alarm underneath her calm tones. They didn't often get unexpected visitors at Bleneccle Manor in the winter; a lone rider was most often the knell of bad news.

There was something familiar about both the man and the horse. Still, it wasn't until he was dismounting that Margot recognized him as Mr. Robbins, her steward from Corinium Park.

Now alarm prickled Margot's skin, too. She hadn't answered Mr. Robbins's most recent letters, but that should not have induced the man to leave Wickhamshire. Whatever brought him on a five days' journey to Bleneccle Manor could not possibly be good.

Setting aside her embroidery, Margot excused herself from the morning room and hurried to the foyer. It was horribly gauche to greet one's steward at the front door, of course, but Margot never set much store by custom at Bleneccle Manor, and besides, she worried he carried news of devastation.

"Mr. Robbins, this is unexpected," she said by way of greeting as the butler admitted him. "I do hope you are well."

Mr. Robbins nodded his head in a bow. He was a short, sturdy man of about fifty, with peppery silver hair that curled rebelliously from beneath the brim of his hat. He'd been with the family since before Geoff was born and had been steward of Corinium Park for twenty years. Even though he was always perfectly polite, Margot had the sensation he thought her a silly ornament to the family, an impression that had only strengthened in the past months when he'd written long letters explaining the state of affairs in Wickhamshire. He was careful to ask her permission, but he never left room for her opinions.

Now, before the man had a chance to respond to Margot, another voice boomed into the room. "So you're Robbins! My man told me you were on the road. Thought you'd gotten snowed in by the storm."

Margot turned to stare at her father. He was in good humor that morning, smiling as if he'd just told a joke, and he bustled past her to greet Mr. Robbins with a congenial tap on the shoulder.

"We'll get you a nice hot brandy to nip the cold right out of you, and then let's settle down to discuss whatever has brought you on such a journey." For Margot, Lord Eastley had only a wink. "Not to worry, my love. I'll take this in hand."

Her father was trying to be kind, she knew. She'd come here to hide from all of the pressures of Corinium Park; he was only trying to shelter her as she'd asked. But as he swept down the corridor with Mr. Robbins, with barely another look at her, Margot couldn't help but feel wronged.

She was the Dowager Countess, after all. Whatever calamity had befallen Corinium Park, Margot needed to know about it – even if she didn't want to. She hadn't had the slightest clue that Mr. Robbins was traveling north, yet her father didn't even seem surprised to see the man. He should have told her whatever he'd known.

And he should have invited her to join the conversation now.

Squaring her shoulders, Margot decided there was only one thing to do. She marched down the hallway after them and barged into the study.

Her father and Mr. Robbins were still on their feet. They were not alone, either; Fitz and Lord Gresham stood around, too, evidently in the middle of being introduced. All eyes turned to Margot, in varying expressions of confusion, dismay, and – from Fitz – a hint of pleasure.

"Lady Wickham." Her father said it quickly, as though he could sense she was about to say something outrageous and wanted to nip it in the bud. "His Grace and Lord Gresham are kind enough to listen in and advise on whatever is troubling Mr. Robbins. You're not to worry."

So he found it fit to share her business with two disinterested lords but meant to shut her out in the meantime.

It was enough to flame her into anger. However, Margot knew better than to give into that fury just yet. Allowing herself only to raise her eyebrows, Margot corrected him, "I'm not worried. I'm interested."

Her father's face reddened. Margot was committing several cardinal sins, including willfully ignoring his wishes and causing an embarrassment in front of guests. Well, he was committing a cardinal sin for her, so she didn't mind giving him a taste of his own medicine. She was bracing for his next argument when a deep, amicable voice disrupted the silence.

"Excellent. You may have my seat, Lady Wickham. My legs would prefer to stand for a while."

Fitz wasn't quite smiling as he said this, but he offered the chair with a friendly, relaxed nonchalance that felt like a grin. Thanking him, Margot took the seat before her father could work out a way to stop her. Fitz remained behind her, leaning against the bookcase. He wasn't improperly close, and yet she could feel his presence as surely as if he had rested a palm on her shoulder. Or tucked his hand inside hers.

They hadn't spoken privately since the kiss. Margot wasn't sure they should. She wasn't sure she *could* speak to him, without throwing herself at him again, begging for another kiss like a woman yearning for water after wandering the desert for years.

Still, she was comforted to have him nearby.

"Fine," her father conceded, taking his own seat behind the desk. Lord Gresham sank into a chair near the hearth, while Mr. Robbins stayed on his feet, gray hat clutched in his hands. "Now, Robbins, what brings you away from Corinium Park?"

"It's the Luddites, my lord." As an afterthought, Mr. Robbins turned his head to include Margot in his address. "As I've mentioned in my letters, for the past few months, we've heard of men in the area taking secret oaths to bring down the new looms. Over in Shropshire, they set fire to the mill just before Christmas. Whispers are that our mill is next. Problem is, the militia went home for the winter. We need the Lord Lieutenant to petition General Dundas to send the regiment back to protect the mill."

Despair – or perhaps it was fear – nipped at Margot. As if the dreadful mill weren't enough, there was the detestable role of Lord Lieutenant settled on her shoulders. Little George, of course, was the true Earl of Wickham, which came with the role of mustering and commanding the local militia, but until he was grown, it all came down to her.

She remembered now why she had been so eager to hand all this over to her father. But she was a different Margot than she'd been in November. She refused to cower in the face of all that overwhelmed her.

"Certainly," her father was saying. "I'll write to General Dundas to request a regiment directed to Wickhamshire."

Margot knitted her fingers in her lap. "That seems rather drastic, considering nothing has happened to our mill yet."

Mr. Robbins set her with the expression he always used and which she so hated—placid eyes with lines of impatience about his mouth. "Perhaps I may inform my lady of the history of the Luddites. They are small-minded men whose sole goal is to wreak havoc on mills."

Margot cut him off before he could continue his

condescension. "I am well aware of the Luddites' history, Mr. Robbins, and I object to the way you characterize them. Weavers have been comfortable families for generations. It is hardly a surprise they would be upset that new looms have replaced them and pay a fraction of what they used to earn. I daresay *you* would be angry should your livelihood suddenly disappear."

"Of course." The man bowed his head, a grimace on his face. "However, perhaps I may remind my lady that the Wickhamshire mill represents a large portion of the Wharton family economy. It has been my duty to your husband and his father before him to protect such investments."

"Quite right," Lord Eastley chimed in. "You do an excellent job. Wharton only ever had praise for his Mr. Robbins."

Said steward nodded his thanks to her father, then skewered Margot with one last grimace. "Further, my lady, Shropshire is only fifty miles from Wickhamshire. I have no doubt the Luddites are mingling in the woods. What happened in Shropshire will happen at any moment in Wickhamshire."

Now both Robbins and her father were staring at her, as if daring her to speak back one more time. Margot wanted to scream back, just to prove she could, but at the same time, she had no more slippery words to throw their way. They knew more than she did; as much as she claimed to know about the Luddites, she'd hardly spent time studying the subject. She was just a silly woman try-ing to insert herself in the middle of a crisis.

She was about to acquiesce, perhaps even to excuse herself to the morning room, when from behind her, Fitz drawled, "What did happen in Shropshire? The reports I read said it was a small fire in the corner of one room. No machinery was damaged. In fact, I don't believe there is any evidence that the Luddites were involved at all."

Mr. Robbins reddened. "One doesn't need evidence when one *knows*, Your Grace. There wasn't any damage only because the foreman happened to be there and threw water on the fire before it could spread."

"Everyone agrees it was the Luddites," Lord Eastley said. "Wharton had been monitoring the situation since '08 when he opened the mill. His greatest fear was that the looms would be destroyed."

Margot hated it when her father mentioned Geoff, mostly because he almost always revealed something new about her husband. How was it that Geoff had confided in his father-in-law more than his wife? And how could his worst fear be for ugly old looms?

"I imagine so," Fitz murmured, "yet I don't see why calling in the militia is your next move. The presence of the militia only makes people angrier. Look at what happened in the Gordon Riots."

"What would you do, then?" her father said, a bit too much of challenge in his tone.

Margot didn't dare turn to look at Fitz, so she had to

content herself with imagining his facial expressions as he spoke. The rise in his eyebrows, the sharpness of his gaze, the softening of his lips.

"If it were my property, my first act would be to visit. One cannot make such a drastic decision without measuring the local mood with one's own senses. From there, I would look for solutions other than calling in the militia. Most Luddites are looking for concessions from the government to protect them. Perhaps there is a solution that doesn't require violence."

"Mr. Robbins is here to represent the local mood. My daughter with her two young children cannot possibly stay alone in Wickhamshire, especially not when there is such agitation in the area." Lord Eastley was looking close to a thunder, yet he reined in his voice. "I hear your points, Your Grace, but I'm afraid we cannot be too careful in this instance. Robbins, I'll write to General Dundas by tomorrow's post. I imagine you may count on a militia no later than next month."

There was a part of her – a dark, childish part – that wanted to leave it be. Her father knew what he was doing. Why should she interfere?

But the larger part of Margot objected. It was one thing for her father to help advise Mr. Robbins on crop plantings or on handling a tenant issue. It was another for him to invoke the powers of Lord Lieutenant on her behalf.

And so she stood. "I should like some time to think it over before agreeing. After all, *I* am the one who must write to General Dundas. I will give you my answer in the morning, in time to get a letter on the mail coach."

Margot waited long enough to see her father's face turn purple with rage. If she stayed any longer, she would regret her words. No, she already regretted them. If she stayed any longer, he would make her take them back. She turned her back to him and Mr. Robbins and Lord Gresham. The last person she saw in the room was Fitz, who smiled.

She didn't have time to think about that. She was too busy retreating, racing up the stone stairs to the sanctuary of her room. Margot had just reclaimed her power, and now she didn't know what to do with it.

Chapter Nine

Fitz spent the afternoon roaming the castle in hopes of "crossing paths" with Margot. She hadn't appeared at luncheon, and he rather feared she planned to stay shut up in her rooms for the rest of the day. He wouldn't blame her. After she had swept out of the study, Fitz had quivered a little himself at the prospect of staying shut up with Winpole. The man could blow the whole castle down with the force of his bellows. To be the one receiving that fury – well, Fitz wouldn't blame Margot if she chose to wait out the storm in her rooms.

Still, he hoped for a private word. For one thing, he wanted to commend her on a job well done. She'd more than held her own in that conversation, even with her father thundering at her and the Robbins man staring down his nose at her.

More importantly, Fitz wanted to persuade her not to take her father's advice.

The question of the Luddites had popped up not infrequently in the ten years since Fitz had first taken his seat in Parliament. Ever since the advent of the spinning jenny, weavers had been petitioning the government for protection: first to outlaw such machines and then to provide protection for their wages. If one took the time to think of the issue from their perspective, their arguments were perfectly logical. Yet the petitions were always accompanied by rumors like the ones Mr. Robbins carried north: a rebellion was brewing that must be quelled.

Fitz made a point of ignoring rumors accompanied by no solid evidence. It didn't surprise him that Winpole would react to anti-Luddite whispers, but he feared that ultimately, Margot would accede to her father's opinion.

If she made up her mind to call in the militia after a round of healthy debate, that was one thing. But Fitz worried she would give in simply because Lord Eastley was her father, and that wouldn't do for a matter so great as bringing soldiers to the doors of her people.

It was all moot if he couldn't find her, of course. He'd stalked the morning room, drawing room, sitting room, and gallery; he'd ducked his head into the kitchen; he'd shrugged into his greatcoat and trudged over to the stables; she was nowhere to be found in the public parts of the manor. Which meant he could either give up or intrude.

That was how he found himself at the nursery, a slim volume of *Yvain, The Knight of the Lion* in his hand.

The scene before him was quite unlike any he was used to. Little Wharton galloped about the room, wooden sword in hand, evidently pretending to be both horse and knight. Trailing after him was the girl – Valentina, if Fitz remembered correctly – calling out in sounds too vague to be words. A castle, built of wooden blocks, stood in the corner by the window, and as Fitz watched, the young earl attacked a pile of blankets that he declared a dragon.

At the center of it all sat Margot, hands behind her back as if she'd been captured. She'd changed into a loose, pearl gray afternoon dress, which did absolutely nothing to highlight her figure and everything to make it easy for her to writhe on the floor, urging her knight to fight a courageous battle. Yet still Fitz could see the outline of a knee, the swell of a breast, and he had to remind his body he was *not* there for another kiss.

Fitz had no memory of ever being in a nursery so lively. He certainly had no memory of his mother getting on the floor to play with him. His nursery had been filled with portraits of his predecessors, not toys for the imagination.

There were, he supposed, advantages to either approach.

Margot noticed him just as Wharton galloped over to free her from invisible chains. With a little gasp, she shot to her feet. "Your Grace, I didn't see you. George, stop, we have a visitor." This last aside was to her son, who turned to gawk at Fitz with huge, curious eyes. The little girl followed her brother's lead, staring as if a giant were invading their forest.

As a rule, Fitz no more than tolerated children. What he intended to do was offer them a curt bow, then speak to their mother. Yet somehow, as they gaped at him with mouths hanging open in perfect ovals, Fitz found himself addressing them. "I'm terribly sorry, I didn't mean to interrupt your adventure. Is the lady saved?"

Wharton pointed his sword at the pile of blankets. "I

killed the dragon!"

"Take Valentina back to the castle now." Margot stepped away from the children to meet Fitz at the threshold. "Did you mean to find your way to the nursery, Your Grace?"

He wished she would quit calling him that, though he supposed she did so to set a good example for the children. Her hair was mussed from the frenzy of play, frizzy and loose in all the wrong places, and there was a brightness to her eyes he hadn't seen before. He wanted her to call him Fitz and swing her arms about his neck and plaster him with kisses.

He cleared his throat. "I found this in my library and thought young Wharton might enjoy it."

Margot took the book with a smile of surprise. "How kind of you. I'm sure George will love it."

Her eyes were so luminous, honey brown irises threaded with gold, that Fitz forgot he had another purpose. It took Margot raising her eyebrow for him to emerge from his cloud.

"I hoped we could speak. Perhaps take a turn around the grounds, or..." He was about to suggest the gallery when he thought better of it. As much as he would like to kiss her again, he didn't want her to misconstrue his invitation as some sort of overture.

"Have you seen our parapets yet?" she suggested.

They sent for their coats. Margot kissed each child's forehead with a reminder to behave, then led Fitz to the tower that rose above the morning room. As soon as they stepped out, Fitz could tell Margot had suggested the antithesis of the gallery. The winter wind was so bitter, only a fool could think of kissing in the midst of it.

He supposed he was getting a little foolish, because even with the whistling gusts, he wanted to taste Margot again.

A wide stone path ringed the tower along the crenellated parapet rising to Fitz's waist. Margot played hostess for a few minutes, chatting about the silver crescent of lake they could see to the east, the mountains rising in somber green-grays to the west, the fields and woods stretching on the other sides. Fitz followed her narration, though at the moment he hadn't much interest in livestock or crops or even summer walks along the lake. She was chattering out of nerves, he supposed, and interrupting might only make her more uncomfortable.

Margot trailed off after a tangent on how a ewe had once chased her into the woods. Laughing a little at herself, she turned to face Fitz. "You didn't want privacy to hear about my troubles with sheep."

"No, although it is a charming story." Fitz rubbed his hands together against the chill air. He paused, hoping to select the perfect words, but Margot spoke first.

"Thank you for intervening earlier. I don't think my father would have let me stay if it hadn't been for you."

"Mr. Robbins should have been speaking to you in the first place."

Margot grimaced, though it was perhaps from a sharp whistle of wind that swept in from the fields. "My father has been kind enough to advise me on most matters since my husband died. I haven't had much interest in it, to tell the truth."

"Duty rarely cares whether one has an interest in it or not."

"Too true. I have had the good fortune to pass off my duty for a time. And I admit, I would dearly love to pass off this particular one, too. I wasn't raised to be a Lord Lieutenant, after all." Here, she laughed at herself again. "However, I'm afraid I'm quite firm in my conviction that I must be the one to decide the militia should be called in."

Fitz wondered if she feared his intention was to dissuade her from that notion. "I agree with you. The law does, too. No one but you has the right to petition for the militia to return to Wickhamshire."

She looked at him with those large, luminous eyes, and Fitz nearly lost his train of thought again. The wind had whipped her hair into even more of a frenzy, and she was wrapped up tight in her heavy coat, yet he couldn't bear the thought of looking away.

"What do you think I should do?"

He opened his mouth to repeat what he'd said earlier in the study. Return to Wickhamshire. Evaluate the situation for herself. Instead, he said, "You should listen to yourself, not Mr. Robbins or your father or me."

Margot heaved a sigh of dismay. "But I have nothing

intelligent to say."

"That's not true. You've said more intelligent things in the two days I've known you than most members of Parliament have in years."

He exaggerated with the intention of making her smile. He didn't expect anything more. But Margot not only beamed, she leapt up and kissed him.

Fitz caught her waist, keeping her close so he could kiss her back. She was a great mass of clothes against his great mass of clothes, yet the heat that sparked from their lips reached all the way down Fitz's body. No matter the wind or the freezing temperature; Fitz would happily stay on that tower for the rest of time, if it meant kissing Margot.

Eventually, the kiss came to an end. Margot withdrew first, tucking her hair behind her reddened ears. She murmured, "I'm sorry."

He couldn't think what she had to be sorry about. "Sometimes a good kiss is just what one needs before making a big decision."

This earned him another smile, though it disappeared all too quickly for his taste. "I'm not sure what I think I'm doing, kissing you. I'm still in mourning."

Fitz tucked his hands into the pockets of his greatcoat. "That would be of greater significance if we were discussing matrimony. I'm not looking for a bride, you know."

The words tumbled out awkwardly, all the more so since they were a lie. He would be looking for a bride soon enough. But he couldn't marry a widow with her own entailments, no matter how much he enjoyed their kisses.

Margot narrowed her eyes. "I didn't refer to the custom of mourning. I referred to the fact that I am still recovering from the loss of my husband. You may not be familiar with it, but a husband and wife often have some form of affection for each other."

He'd offended her. Fitz supposed he deserved the tongue lashing. He'd trodden right over her feelings, after all. He took a step back. "Of course. My apologies."

Margot raised her chin. She'd made the exact same gesture in the study just a few hours before, when setting her father and Mr. Robbins in their place. Fitz discovered he preferred to be on the observing end of that look rather than receiving it.

"I should return downstairs," she announced.

"I didn't mean to offend you," Fitz said. "I've said the wrong thing."

Margot settled him with one last glare. "You've clarified your intentions. I thank you. It has helped me clarify mine. Now, if you'll excuse me, I'll see you at dinner."

She swept down the stairs, just in time for a gust of wind to sweep icy chills down Fitz's neck. He watched her go. It was for the best, of course. He didn't want to get too entangled in a new relationship if he was going to recruit a wife in just a few months. And he certainly didn't want to make a mess of Margot's feelings.

Still, he wished he hadn't said it. And he wished she

hadn't left. And he wished he'd never made that stupid bet with Annabelle.

Chapter Ten

Bleneccle Manor was abuzz even before the sun crested the mountains the next morning. Given Mr. Robbins's report that the roads were relatively clear of snow – and the prediction in the almanac that they had three days before another storm – it was decided over dinner that Lord Gresham's party must continue their adventure to the Duke of Surrey's winter home in Derby. They meant to depart just after breakfast, when they would have a good six hours of daylight, and so the household bustled to prepare their trunks and ready their carriage.

Margot kept to her bedchamber, listening to the rushed footfalls of the household from the safety of her window seat. She hadn't slept well – had barely slept at all – with everything that was on her mind. The question of the militia, the question of Fitz, the question of what exactly she was doing...they tumbled around with no answers.

Oh, she found it tiresome to be so lost. A grown woman – a mother of two, no less! – should have only answers, not days smeared with shadows of question marks.

In any case, she reminded herself, she couldn't stall on the question of the militia much longer. The sky was already pink from the sunrise. Soon breakfast would be served, and Mr. Robbins would look for a letter to drop in the post as he rode through town.

Much as she hated to think of militiamen spilling through the green lanes of Wickhamshire, Margot supposed she had better send the letter after all. It would take a month or so for the militia to arrive, in any case, by which time perhaps the threat would disappear. Margot could take Mr. Robbins's advice while still hoping to resolve the issue without violence.

Unless, as Fitz warned, the militia would only make the situation worse.

Oh, Margot was so tired of turning the options over in her head. She needed to make a decision and keep to it, come what may.

And when it came to whom she should be listening to…Margot supposed she was better off relying on her father, who hadn't yet steered her wrong, than some duke who thought he could go kissing anyone in the countryside he wanted to.

No matter that *she* was the one who had kissed him most recently. And whose whole body yearned for more of the same. Fitz clearly didn't think much of it, if he was so quick to remind her he would *not,* in fact, be marrying her.

As if she were looking for another husband. Margot had experienced quite enough of matrimony for a lifetime. She didn't need to give her heart to some other man who would lose track of it while building a mill or a railroad.

Margot was grateful when a knock on her door interrupted that train of thinking. Alice slipped into the room, joining her to perch on the cushioned stone bench. Margot's bedchamber had the best view of the lake, always glimmering just beyond reach, and they'd spent hours playing with their dolls in that window seat. Now Alice wrapped an arm around Margot's shoulders.

"Oh dear, is that the old gloom returning over my big sister? I thought you were going to win our little bet."

"Not gloom. Too much on my mind." Margot smiled to prove she could. "So you see, I can still claim the right to name my little niece or nephew. How do you like Satania, for a girl?"

Alice wrinkled her nose. "About our wager, I'm afraid we might have to let it lie unfinished. Hugh thinks we had better return to Richmond Hall while the weather permits. He is afraid we'll be stuck here for my confinement otherwise."

This surprised Margot. Alice had spent the last few months reassuring her that they preferred Bleneccle Manor to Richmond Hall and couldn't bear to leave while Margot was still at home. Though now that Margot thought of it, two months was a long stay when they lived only a few miles away. Alice would want to be fixing up her own home for their child, not moping about the old castle.

"Will you be alright with just Mama and Papa for company?" Alice asked.

"You forget George and Valentina. They are enough company wherever we are." The prospect of an empty Bleneccle Manor was rather gloomy, but Margot wouldn't hold her sister back any more than she already had. "When do you leave?"

"After breakfast, with the rest of the party."

It was so soon, Margot could only imagine they'd been plotting it for days. Poor Alice must have been afraid it would send Margot into a tailspin if she disclosed the news any earlier.

Margot rose. "Then you must declare me the winner of our wager. I am in much improved spirits since our company arrived, as you can see."

"I rather thought we could call it null," Alice protested.

"Nonsense. I have won early, that is all. Why, I'm up and about before the sun."

"So is the whole house."

"I didn't take a single nap in the last two days."

Alice chewed her lower lip. "I suppose you have a point. You have been a good hostess to our guests, as well."

"Was I not the picture of cheer playing whist last night?"

"Indeed. Not to mention what a good flirt you've been with the duke."

Margot grasped at indignation. "I beg your pardon. I have not flirted."

"You cannot deny it. You walked alone with him in the gallery for nearly a quarter of an hour!"

"We were getting air away from the crowded drawing room." Yet she knew her objection rang false. And she couldn't very well argue the point for long, since she had done far worse than merely *flirt* with Fitz.

"I've gotten air with a duke before, Margot. I know what happens next."

"Pray don't presume the Duke of Harrodshire has any-thing in common with the Duke of Cornwall." But Alice's sisterly grin worked its magic, and Margot collapsed back on the window seat to confess. "He did kiss me. But it was nothing as sordid as your little adventure."

"Of course not. You're a widow, not an innocent debu-tante whose reputation can be flung into the gutter. Did you enjoy it?"

Her cheeks grew hot from remembering the kiss. *Enjoy* didn't seem like enough of a word to describe how it had felt to be wrapped in his arms. He'd held her as if he feared he'd drop her.

Likely he kissed all his women that way.

Oh, she didn't have time for silly girlish feelings. She needed to decide about the militia.

"No matter. He's departing this morning, too. The point is that I am much improved, and therefore I have won our wager, even though the week is not yet up."

Alice still smiled. "Very well. I shall apply myself to having a boy, or else a daughter named Satania." Rising, she pressed a kiss to Margot's cheek. "I must return to packing. You had better start working on your farewell speech. I expect it to leave me in tears for a week."

Margot clasped Alice in a hug before letting her go. It had been years since they'd had so much time together, and the first time her little sister had truly felt like a friend and not a nuisance. She hated to say goodbye.

But all good things must come to an end, she reminded herself, ringing for her maid. And the verso of that was true, as well: all tribulations must come to an end. Margot had survived the worst of her grief; she would survive this strange moment as Lord Lieutenant, too.

No matter what Fitz thought of her. No matter that she wasn't quite sure what she wanted to do. Margot had a duty to make the right decision for the people of Wickhamshire, and that was her focus, through and through.

Now if only she could make the decision.

Chapter Eleven

The battle happened at breakfast. It was a brilliant day, nearly balmy compared to the previous wintry cold, and the morning sun shone strongly enough that icicles sweated steadily from the castle's eaves. Mr. Robbins, man of action, was the first to the makeshift table in the morning room; he was already picking at a lone helping of oatmeal when Fitz descended. Next came Talbot and Annabelle, dressed in their traveling costumes.

Fitz girded himself with a heavy plate of three boiled eggs and thick slabs of toast, slathered in fresh butter and jam, to keep him full for a day of riding. He wished they weren't leaving just yet. Margot had been cool to him ever since his blunder on the tower. He wanted an opportunity to apologize again, though he wasn't quite sure what to say.

He only knew he hated to leave while she held him in bad esteem.

Lady Eastley was the next to arrive, filling the room with her beaming presence. In the morning light, Fitz detected Margot's kind, mischievous eyes in Lady Eastley's gentler countenance. He regretted that he hadn't spent more time acquainting himself with her.

In his typical fashion, Lord Eastley entered loudly, landing a slap on Robbins's shoulder. "Lucky it's a good day for travel, eh?"

Margot took forever to arrive. Fitz, seated with a view of the doorway, kept glancing up, hoping the butler or the serving maid or even a shadow would reveal itself as she. Annabelle, in the midst of telling a story about Spanish breakfasts, needled, "Am I boring you, Fitz?"

He gave her his most charming smile. "It's only that I've heard this story already, my dear Lady Gresham."

"Phooey. I haven't told this story in years. I barely remember how it ends." Annabelle waved to the footman. "His Grace needs more tea. He is losing his ability to charm his foot out of his mouth."

Fitz was certainly losing his grasp on subtlety, for even as he accepted the cup of tea, he caught himself looking to the threshold again.

"Perhaps you are looking for someone?" Annabelle murmured this time. "Your favorite widow?"

He hoped he did not blush. At the moment, he didn't give a fig whether Annabelle considered Margot his flirtation. There was too much at stake besides a little wager. Blast whatever it was he wanted to say to Margot. This was the moment when she would announce her decision. He was sitting upon thorns wondering whether she would follow her father's advice or not. He wanted to be helpful, whatever she decided.

If that helped him to earn her forgiveness, all the better.

Margot finally entered, on the arm of her sister and trailed by Osborne. She wore a simple black gown, its neck modestly scooped high above her bosom, and her hair shook in a curled frame around her face. Fitz allowed himself one inhale to admire the perfect slope of her nose and curve of her lips.

Then he returned his attention to the table.

Talbot was discussing their journey for the morning. "We should have plenty of daylight to make it to town and evaluate road conditions. Mr. Robbins, you said the snow was packed down enough for a carriage?"

The steward nodded. "Certainly on the highway. The stretch today, between the manor and town, might be the worst of it, if you ask me."

"Since you're a lone rider, Robbins, you'll go ahead to town and alert the inn to expect His Grace's party," Lord Eastley said. "That way there'll be a hot bath awaiting Lady Gresham no matter how long the journey."

Fitz looked to Margot, who was just sitting down with a plate of sausage and eggs. Her lips tightened into a thin line, but otherwise, she gave no indication of even hearing the conversation, much less having an opinion.

"Certainly, sir." Robbins wiped his mouth with the back of his hand. "Of course, I'll still be needing that letter to General Dundas before I go."

"Yes, you'll have it." Lord Eastley turned to Fitz. "Perhaps Your Grace would like to add a letter in support of the request, to expedite the approval?"

An interesting approach. Fitz supposed Winpole was wise enough to realize he didn't have the legal power to request the deployment of a militia to Wickhamshire. Fitz nodded without commitment. "If it is what Lady Wickham wishes."

The energy around the table stilled as all eyes landed on Margot. A slight flush crept up her neck, but she raised her chin like a queen anyway. Fitz flicked away the tickle of desire at his base as she announced, "After more thought, I would prefer to return to Wickhamshire and evaluate the situation myself before taking any specific measures."

Watching the reactions of everyone other than Winpole and Robbins, Fitz noted the mixture of surprise and pride in Lady Eastley's eyes, and approval in Annabelle's smile. Lord and Lady Windemere slid their eyes to each other, as smoothly as a choreographed dance, while Talbot simply reached for more tea.

Robbins was the first to speak. "Beg your pardon, my lady, but by the time you evaluate the situation, it may be too late."

Before the steward could even finish his sentence, Lord Eastley was sputtering. "Return to Wickhamshire? Evaluate the situation? Don't be daft, Margot. You'll stay here, safe and sound, and let Robbins do his job."

Margot's gaze fluttered downward. "George is the Earl of Wickham, and I am the Dowager Countess until he is of age. It is my duty to return and make the decision for myself."

"No, it is your duty to keep your son safe." Winpole started cutting the sausage on his plate into smaller and smaller pieces. "You wouldn't even know what to evaluate once you got there. Have you any inkling how to detect whether a riot is about to erupt? No. That's why we pay Mr. Robbins to look after things for us. Your presence is neither necessary nor wise."

"*I* pay Mr. Robbins, not *we*." Margot said it so softly, Fitz wasn't sure her father had heard.

Until the older man thundered back, "*You* don't pay anything. It is all George's money. You're merely his care-taker until he is old enough to monitor it himself. As your father, it is my responsibility to monitor it for you, so that you don't do anything daft like giving it all to the Luddites instead of calling in the militia."

Throwing her napkin on the table, Margot turned in horror to her father. "I never said anything of the sort! Furthermore, the moment I married Geoff, I stopped being your responsibility. I appreciate you letting us visit for so long, but it is really time that I return with my children to our home. In Wickhamshire."

"Margot, you are overtired. Go back to bed, and we'll discuss this more later."

At this, Lady Eastley glared daggers at her husband, but Margot shot to her feet anyway. "There is nothing more to discuss. Mr. Robbins, my children and I will travel back with you."

"Using whose carriage?" Winpole bellowed. "You don't have your own here, and since you're not my responsibility, I know you won't be in one of mine."

Now Annabelle spoke up, in that friendly, melodic way of hers. "I do hate to intrude on family discord, but Lady Wickham is always welcome to travel with us. There's room enough if some of us ride the horses. Isn't that right, Lord Gresham?"

Talbot looked about ready to melt with embarrassment, but he managed a nod. Fitz suppressed a grin.

"There. It's fixed. We'll all travel south together." Margot strutted towards the door. "I'll be ready in an hour. Don't you dare leave without me, Mr. Robbins."

The poor steward looked fit for a heart attack from the argument. He whispered too loudly to Lord Eastley, "Could I still have a letter in support of the militia, my lord?"

Margot turned on her heel. Looming in the threshold with a billowing skirt and burning eyes, she was the picture of authority. "You will not have that letter, Mr. Robbins."

"Of course you will have the letter, Mr. Robbins," Winpole hissed.

"I'll rip it up," Margot said.

"I'll write him multiple copies." Winpole stood, meeting his daughter in the threshold to tower over her.

She jutted her chin forward. "I'll find them all. I'll burn every last one."

"I'll send the letter directly to General Dundas."

"Fine." Margot didn't take her eyes off her father as she threatened, "His Grace will write to the general to contradict your request."

Lord Eastley turned his raging red face to Fitz. "Your Grace wouldn't interfere on a family matter."

Fitz felt the power of every eye in the room on him, from Winpole all the way down to the footman. The only gaze he really cared about was Margot's, which was currently raw and triumphant.

She knew what he would say next.

Standing, Fitz folded his napkin carefully onto the table. "Lord Eastley, while I know that you are acting out of a father's best intentions, my allegiances lie with the country and with the proper alignment of responsibilities. On principle, I believe the decision is Lady Wickham's alone. Furthermore, in substance, calling the militia is a drastic precedent to set. I fear you must, as a father, trust that Lady Wickham has learned your sound judgment and let her make the ruling."

Winpole deflated. Where just a moment before he had been a red-faced, puffed up old man, now his shoulders sagged, and he looked only gray and tired.

Fitz felt a little bad for him. "If it would bring you any comfort, since we will already be traveling together, I would be happy to accompany Lady Wickham to Wickhamshire and offer my guidance on the situation."

It was hardly a sacrifice to offer. True, it would delay him from returning to his own seat by another week or two, but Fitz supposed Margot really could use the help, considering her confession that she had been relying so heavily on her father's advice of late. Besides, it meant that many more days in her company.

Fitz was so busy anticipating the cozy room arrangements at an inn that he almost missed Margot's reaction to his offer. He saw only Lord Eastley, looking a little calmer, nodding with a smile.

But in the last moment, he glanced at Margot. Just in time to see anger flame anew in her eyes.

Chapter Twelve

Margot's fury crystallized into a cool, numb certainty. At some deep level, she still shook, but skating above it, she clung to what she knew: she didn't like the way Mr. Robbins kept looking to her father for direction, she didn't like Fitz inviting himself to oversee her at her own home, and she hated the way her father had yelled at her.

She hated being yelled at, and she hated what he'd said to her.

Margot welcomed the cloak of numbness that fell across her chest as she raced from the morning room to the children's chambers. She held it close as she directed Nurse to have the children ready to leave within the hour. She tied it tighter as she refused her father's belated offer to use his carriage. She was grateful it kept her from crying as she kissed her mother goodbye.

It took them the whole afternoon to travel the bumpy, icy four miles into town. Robbins went ahead on his horse, while Fitz rode alongside the carriage on his own mare. The rest of them squeezed into the carriage. It was a luxurious carriage, both the bench and its back padded generously, and the windows lined with velvet curtains to keep the warmth in. But between Lord and Lady Gresham, Margot, Nurse, and the children, its luxury quickly felt nothing but crowded.

Still, Margot was so cool in her certainty that she barely noticed.

They stopped at the town's one inn. The Three Cups had been run by Mr. and Mrs. Armstrong for as long as Margot could remember. As George raced around the courtyard, delighted at his new freedom, Margot tamped down surging memories of her own family's trips through The Three Cups. She didn't need to remember how her father and Mr. Armstrong had always greeted each other like long-lost brothers, chatting about the harvest as if they were both tenant farmers, nor how Mrs. Armstrong had always brewed a special hot milk for Margot and Alice to help them sleep full and sound.

Instead, she focused on the fluster of who would have which bed. The Three Cups only had three rooms, and here they were, a group of eight. The Armstrongs had already sorted out Mr. Robbins, who would stay with the baker down the lane. Nurse would share the room under the eaves with George and Valentina. That left two rooms for Annabelle, Talbot, Margot, and Fitz.

Annabelle, overhearing the issue, turned to Margot. "That's settled, then, isn't it? You and I will be bed partners tonight, and Fitz will be the one to put up with Bernie's snoring."

Talbot turned red all the way to the tips of his ears, but he grinned along. "I hope His Grace has learned to share the quilt."

Mrs. Armstrong, satisfied, bustled them into the private dinner room for wine and stew before bed. Annabelle hooked her arm through Margot's, whispering, "And if you prefer a bed swap, we can arrange it once the tavern's asleep."

Now it was Margot's turn to flush, despite the cloak that stopped her heart from quickening. She glanced at Fitz behind them, who hadn't heard the comment. His lips twitched into a smile as he caught her eyes.

The devil in duke's clothes. Why else would he urge her to follow her own instincts, only to insert himself as her new supervisor?

She turned back to Annabelle. "That will not be necessary."

Valentina stole the show at supper, wailing her whole lungs out as Nurse tried to feed her stew. Mrs. Armstrong offered to remove the children to the kitchen, but Fitz issued a ducal decree before anyone else could speak. "Let them stay."

His eyes drifted to Margot, his face carefully expressionless. Margot surmised she was supposed to react, to crumble in gratitude for this man who welcomed chaos merely because they were her children.

Another night, she might have. But that cloak still hung heavy on her shoulders, and Margot felt only confusion.

She retired with the children, ostensibly to help Nurse put them to bed but really because she was feeling that bone-deep exhaustion that had defined so much of the past six months. Perhaps she had been too quick to crow over Alice that she had won the wager. All it took was one terrible argument to knock her back into the depths of grief.

Margot nestled herself between the children on their slim shared mattress and told them fairy stories until they finally drifted into sleep. George's sleepy breath fluttered hot against her chest. Margot studied his profile, his tender little cheeks and perfect tiny nose. One day, she knew, he wouldn't be so small. One day, he would tower over her, and he would be sure of his opinions just like her father and Fitz and Mr. Robbins.

He would set her down, from Dowager Countess to his old mother, and he would ignore her advice and he would bring in a wife to do the entertaining, and Margot would be a shadow.

But she loved him. She wanted George to be that man, the one who would rise to his duties like a general to his command. She forgave him already for all the ways he would diminish her because it was his destiny.

Margot wondered if that meant she had to forgive her father, too.

Leaving her children and Nurse to their peace, Margot crossed the hall into the bedroom intended for her and Annabelle. It was what Mrs. Armstrong referred to as "The Mistress's Room," always saved for Lady Eastley when Margot's parents traveled. The mattress – a fine horsehair pallet that Lady Eastley had gifted the inn a decade ago – sat on a cherry-wood frame high above the woven carpet. Along one wall sat a fat, painted armoire and a matching wash table with an oval mirror and porcelain jug and basin. Since Margot's last visit, the whitewashed walls had been updated with a hand-painted rose vine circling the room.

The room, so cheerful, usually brought a smile to Margot's face. Now, she sank into the chair beside the wash table, feeling lost. For something to do, she released her hair from its arrangement and started pulling her brush through, counting the strokes. Her goal was one hundred, but then she kept going. The motion was repetitive, and easy, and didn't require any thought. When Annabelle entered, Margot was up to two hundred and forty-three.

"Would you like help braiding your hair?" Annabelle asked.

Margot hadn't thought that far ahead. "Thank you."

Annabelle's fingers were thin and nimble as they pulled Margot's hair back into a long, loose braid. Margot wondered how a duchess could be so good at playing abigail, but she didn't ask, instead watching the lady in the mirror. Catching her, Annabelle smiled. "How long have you been in mourning?"

"Seven months."

Annabelle nodded. "I was so tired of wearing black by that point. Of course, mine wasn't a love match, so my heart wasn't broken."

"Mine was a love match, but my heart was broken

long before he died," Margot said, before she caught herself. "Still, life seemed much simpler when Lord Wickham was alive. I suppose he made all the difficult decisions, while I thought choosing whom to visit each afternoon was complex."

"It *is* complex when there are personalities and egos involved. If there was one thing I learned in all those years traveling the continent, meeting all the kings and princes I could name, it is that when a shrewd woman hosts the right people at the right time, there will be peace."

Margot hardly felt managing the alliances of her neighbors was as important as managing the alliances of neighboring countries. Still, she appreciated Annabelle's efforts.

"You know, I was quite impressed with you this morning," she went on. "It is no easy thing to stand up to one's father. But you are the Dowager Countess, not he. You have every right to make the decisions yourself. You should be proud that you found that courage."

It didn't feel like courage to Margot. Not in the moment, when her whole body quaked as her father bellowed. Nor now, hours later, when she knew she couldn't possibly make any decisions herself. She couldn't even braid her own hair.

"I didn't mean to. I was going to propose that we travel home *and* that Papa write to General Dundas. But then he started being so obstinate that I refused the letter out of spite." Margot lifted her shoulders in shame. "Besides, he wouldn't have let me leave had Fitz not said he'd travel with us."

"One must use whatever weapons one has. If you have Fitz in your quiver, you would be a fool not to use him." Annabelle finished the braid, tying it off with one of Margot's discarded silk ribbons.

"Perhaps." Margot turned on her little chair the better to face her. "But then Fitz erected another wall by saying he would come to Wickhamshire. He might as well have declared he will make the decision for me."

Annabelle tilted her head at this, blue eyes glittering in the firelight. "I rather thought he was trying to find a reason to stay by your side longer."

Margot blushed. Annabelle clearly knew something was passing between her and Fitz. She wondered if she should confess to the kisses, the better to understand what she wanted from them.

Before she could say another word, there was a knock at the door. Margot answered it, worrying it might be Nurse come to report a problem with the children.

Instead, it was Talbot and Fitz. "I wondered if I might beg of my wife to play valet for the evening," Talbot said, clearing his throat as his gaze raked over said female. "I am at a loss as to how to free my neck of this tie, and His Grace the Duke of Harrodshire refuses to help."

Annabelle smiled, the perfect lady. "As you bid, my liege."

Fitz lingered at the threshold as they swanned into

the next room. He set those gray eyes on her, as if they had known each other forever. "I couldn't help but notice that you've been quiet. Are you feeling all right?"

Margot wanted to bristle and retort with something clever. But his question was too kind, and she was too tired. "I'm afraid today has been exhausting in every way."

He stepped forward. It was only a few inches, yet suddenly Margot could smell him – the hay and leather and horse, the rich stew, the yeasty ale. She remembered what it felt like to be held in his arms, to press against his chest, to feel the whole world disappear as he swept her into a kiss.

She inched a step backward.

"Would you like to talk about it?" Fitz asked.

"No." She truly didn't. But then, when her answer made Fitz look away – a flicker of hurt leaping through his eyes – that cloak of numbness loosened. Just enough anger and curiosity surged forward for her to ask, "Why did you bait me into arguing with my father only to proclaim yourself my new lord and master?"

Fitz jerked his gaze back to her. "I did no such thing."

"You might as well have when you announced you would travel with me to Wickhamshire and 'supervise' my decision."

Fitz straightened, somehow growing even more tall and ducal. "It was a simple compromise to bring a resolution to the discussion. It was an outcome your father would accept because you would not be alone in Wickhamshire.

It was an outcome you would accept – I thought - because you do not find my company objectionable. My apologies if I miscalculated."

Margot refused to be distracted by the cold vulnerability in his words. "My father accepted it because he thinks *you* will be making the decision."

"Does it matter why he accepted it? You have the outcome you desired." Fitz leaned forward, resting a hand on the doorframe. "I strike compromises like this in Parliament all the time. Otherwise we would never get anything done."

"The Diplomatic Duke in action." Margot spit the words to show how unimpressed she was. "You failed to consider whether I would be satisfied with the outcome you so deftly engineered. You were the one who told me it was my decision to make. I'm not going to forget that simply because you are now He who whispers in my ear."

For a moment, all Fitz did was stare at her, anger etched into his brow. Then he surprised her. He placed his hand over his heart. "I apologize. I truly didn't mean it that way. If I may be honest, I saw only an opportunity to prolong our friendship. I'll leave you before we reach Wickhamshire, if that's what you wish."

Margot wasn't used to apologies, not in the middle of an argument. It was enough to push that cloak all the way off. She might as well have been naked, her emotions shivering bare on her heart.

There was only one thing to do. It was, she realized,

what she had longed to do since the moment she opened the door and saw Fitz behind Talbot. Or perhaps before – since they had disembarked at the inn, or maybe even since that morning when her father had tried to bellow a cage around her.

She threw herself into Fitz's arms. His chest was wide and solid, and her head nestled at just the top of his shoulder. He wrapped his arms across her back, holding her strong and firm in his orbit.

It was not sensual, just a hug that rooted Margot back to the ground. When she stepped back, it was because her heart had finally stopped quaking at every breath.

And then their eyes connected. In Fitz's eyes, she saw a jumble of joy and fear and desire. Margot surged upward this time, palming the back of his neck to bring his lips to hers.

The kiss was all the sweeter for their argument. It sparked straight from Margot's lips down to the center of her desires, heating her body in one fell stroke. Fitz's hands shifted on her back, pressing her close so she could feel his response. She hadn't felt a man's excitement against her in too long. Her body softened, melting against him, ready for the evening to disappear into this kiss.

Margot could spend eternity kissing Fitz, their lips the center of the world.

But they still stood in the doorway. If they carried on much further, Margot would need to invite him into the bedroom. And she was quite sure she didn't want to do that.

As much as Margot's thoughts danced around their kiss, it was Fitz who pulled away. "You see why I am so eager to visit you in Wickhamshire?"

Margot smiled. It was, perhaps, her first smile of the day. "If this is the reason, I am eager to play your hostess."

They held onto each other for a few heartbeats more, then separated for good. Fitz retreated to the tavern, while Margot shut the door and prepared for bed. Now her thoughts were jumbled for new reasons.

Mostly good reasons, this time.

Annabelle returned soon after, looking only slightly more rumpled than when she had exited.

"Did you sort everything out with Fitz, then?"

Margot smiled. "For the most part. Were you able to manage Lord Gresham's tie?"

The lady grinned wickedly.

Changed into their nightshifts, their legs banged against each other as they settled into their spots, and they giggled over the new intimacy.

Annabelle blew out the bedside candle, so the room only glowed softly from the coal embers in the fireplace. She whispered, "Will you lend me some of your courage when we get to Derby?"

"Whatever do you need courage for?" Margot couldn't picture the equanimous lady quivering in any situation.

Annabelle tugged the quilt all the way up to her chin. "The new Duke of Surrey is more a King George than a Prince Regent, if you see what I mean. A stickler for propriety. He never approved of his father marrying me. I came out the same year as his eldest daughter, after all! He expected me to come home and play the part of a bereaved widow. You know, wear the weeds for the rest of my life and never look another man in the eye. Now Talbot and I have eloped…he is not going to be pleased."

Margot had met the man when he was still the viscount. Older than her own father, the new duke still wore his hair in a towering powdered wig and rouged his cheeks before the balls. Worse, his breath stank of spoiled eggs if one got too close to him.

She didn't envy Annabelle her task.

"What does it matter how he reacts? You're already married. He can't do anything about that."

Annabelle heaved a sigh. "My husband left me an annual income, one which we dearly need. It is legally safe and sound, but if the new duke chooses not to honor it, Talbot and I have neither the money nor the social goodwill to take a Surrey to court."

How Margot hated money. Or perhaps it was simply the system of money. Or the fact that it was only ever men who held it.

"So you see, I need some of your courage to even show up at his door."

Under the cover, Margot found Annabelle's hand and gave it a squeeze. "You underestimate yourself. You've dined with kings and princes; one ornery old man is no match for your charm."

Annabelle shivered. "How I wish I could control my own fate, rather than relying on one man or another."

"If we women held the purse strings, the world would be much simpler, wouldn't it?" Margot mused. "There would be enough food for every mouth to eat and a bed for every body to sleep in. No need to marry for money, or worry about not eating if you marry for love."

"If only we have enough income, I mean to do something about that," Annabelle said. "The right party with the right people can move the needle on policy. I've seen it happen. I mean to be the hostess of London gatherings where decisions are made, and those decisions will be about making everyone's lot better."

Margot was surprised by the steel in Annabelle's words, when so far she had been nothing more than the most affable lady in the room.

But just as she noticed it, the charm slipped right back in as Annabelle capped the conversation with, "Enough of that for tonight. Let's rest up for the journey tomorrow."

They whispered final goodnights, then settled into sleeping positions. Margot closed her eyes, willing sleep to come easily. But her mind was caught on Annabelle's vision.

This was a woman who had spent time dreaming of her future, beyond merely planning for this year's Season. Her plans weren't confined to her own little sphere of family or friends. She dreamt of the whole world.

Margot wished she had a dream like that.

Chapter Thirteen

Riding alone on Roona was usually Fitz's favorite way of working out his next moves in Parliament. There was something about fresh country air, the comfort of a horse, and no one else around that let his mind work with more clarity. He'd planned the great compromise of 1808 riding from his ducal seat to London. He'd plotted how to pass the County Asylums Act while riding through the Sherwood Forest.

Now he had countless moves to plan. With the Prince of Wales lined up as the official Regent, there was tension in the air, and tension meant Fitz could get things done. He wanted to start with the domestic, little ways to protect the average Englishman without bucking tradition, such as setting standards for apothecaries and adding more protections for the boy chimneysweeps, who too often got stuck in chimneys. He needed to line up the correct votes in the House of Lords, find allies in the House of Commons, and convince Prinny to support it.

Yet Fitz couldn't seem to stop thinking about Margot. That morning, she had thrown him a little smile as she climbed into the carriage. He would have missed it if he had blinked. Now he replayed it, adding a twinkle to her eye, a lick of her lip, wondering when she would smile at him again. He rode not six feet ahead of the carriage, yet

Margot might as well have been in London. He yearned for their next stop, just to step close to her again.

He shook himself, alarmed at the desperation in his thoughts. Yesterday, she had marched around the house without a word to him about their victory, then shut herself in the carriage without so much as a glare. Then he had chewed over the moments between them, worrying that he had so offended her that she should frost him out.

But today, he was in the clear. They'd straightened everything out and even kissed to seal the deal. What a kiss, too, standing dangerously on the threshold, where anyone might have seen them. Margot had been so earnest, throwing her lips against his, taking from him exactly what she needed. Fitz's paramours were usually seasoned mistresses who followed their own set of rules as faithfully as the debutantes at Almack's. He wasn't accustomed to a woman who simply said what was on her mind and asked for what she wanted.

Fitz took a deep breath of winter air to clear his mind again. This was why he didn't need to be thinking about Margot: they would simply sort out what happened next together, the two of them. Yet still his thoughts circled back to her smile, her lips, her beautiful, supple body. Fitz blamed the northern cold, which was too frigid for thinking important thoughts. The temperature flirted with freezing, though the sun shone warmly enough to heat his shoulders and melt the snow hanging on the tree branches. He had to rub his hands together periodically to keep his fingers from freezing stiff.

No doubt in the carriage, they all huddled close together, sharing the heated bricks. Usually, Fitz would abhor getting so close to his friends for something so base as heat, yet he found himself wishing he were in there, cozying up next to Margot.

And there he went again. Now Fitz tried to be sterner with himself. He focused on creating a mental list of all the peers who would oppose an apothecary bill, and what he could give them to gain their support. But that only brought him back to the argument last night, when Margot had hissed, "The Diplomatic Duke in action," as if it were an epithet.

Was that how everyone felt? Fitz had always prided himself on being able to find middle ground and strike compromises in the name of action. But did others go around town wielding the title as a weapon against him?

Margot certainly hadn't been happy with the compromise he'd made on her behalf. No confrontation with a peer compared to how she made his heart thunder when she'd accused him of usurping her power.

Fitz hoped she'd believed him when he'd sworn that wasn't his intention. He hoped she didn't judge him too harshly that his honest motivation had been more time to get under her skirts.

He himself didn't want to examine that motivation too closely.

And so it went all day. Margot seized his thoughts,

whether he tried to concentrate on Parliament or the matter of his failed wheat harvest that autumn or even the daring birds soaring across the clear sky. The very road reminded him of Margot, for over the course of the day it had flattened into a wide lane through forests and fields; just as she had murmured that first night at dinner, the highway was friendlier if one travelled with a Northerner.

At midday break, he strove to drink up Margot, to get his fill so his mind could focus elsewhere for the afternoon. But she was so preoccupied trying to contain Valentina's pent-up energy – while the nurse raced after Wharton, who ran circles around the tavern – that they barely exchanged two words. Worse, she was enchanting in her gray travel costume, ruffled and anxious and perfectly complex. Now he had a whole afternoon of contemplating motherhood, a subject he had never before considered closely. Instead of solving the question of child chimneysweeps, Fitz instead pondered the nature of love, and whether loving a child came from the same fierce furnace as a man's love for a woman.

Not that he had ever experienced either kind himself.

By the time they reached the inn for the evening, Fitz was thoroughly sick of himself. He didn't want to waste one more second thinking of a woman, no matter how perfect she was. If he spent the evening indulging his baser desires to stay by Margot's side, he would only spend the rest of the journey obsessing about it. No, the only solution was to stay as far from her as possible, the better to cure himself of his hang-up.

The dark was already nestling across the countryside as they dismounted at the Crossing Lions. Shabbier than the Three Cups, this inn was nevertheless larger, boasting seven guest rooms above a tavern spacious enough to host a country dance. The innkeeper, alerted early by Robbins, had the private dining room ready for the ducal party when they arrived, and even had a serving girl available to whisk George and Valentina off to the makeshift nursery.

They set a leather chair at the head of the table for Fitz, as if he were a king who needed a throne. He settled in with a rueful smile, accepting a mug of ale as Talbot and Annabelle sat on his right. Margot was to his left, directly beside him. When she first sat down, her boots brushed his, and they both jumped, as if sparked by electricity.

Fitz turned to Talbot. "Ready to leave the carriage to the females? I'm sure we can hire a horse for you to ride tomorrow."

"I'm not interested in freezing my bollocks off, if you'll pardon my language, Lady Wickham."

"It's not so bad," Fitz said, though he still hadn't completely regained feeling in his fingertips despite the warm fleece-lined gloves he had worn all day. "Besides, I've got business to talk with you."

"If this is about your apothecary bill, I've already written Montberry about it as you asked." Turning, Talbot stage-whispered to the ladies, "His Grace is as much a nag as my grandmother."

The innkeeper entered with his wife, serving earthenware urns of mutton stew and fresh hot loaves of bread. Fitz stole a glimpse of Margot, despite himself, relishing in the flush of her cheeks as she breathed in the heavenly smell of food.

Before he remembered to look away, she lifted her brown eyes to him. "What is your apothecary bill?"

Fitz weighed the question. On the one hand, it was impolite to discuss politics in the presence of ladies. On the other hand, she was the one broaching the subject. And it might help him get his mind back on track.

"If you have a fever and cough, your housekeeper might give you a hot compress. A physician might give you a bottle of morphine. A pharmacist might give you a serum. What stops the innkeeper from bottling this stew and selling it for a shilling as a new miracle medicine?"

Margot took a bite of said stew. "A proper upbringing?"

Fitz lifted his hands in thanks. "Precisely. There is no regulation around who is qualified to provide medicine. Hence charlatans charging ridiculous sums for 'miracle cures,' and worse, offering up 'medicines' that harm rather than heal. I propose a bill that certifies proper apothecaries."

"Why must Talbot write to Montberry?" Margot asked, her gaze drifting across the table to Talbot. "Surely there is no reason to oppose such a bill."

Fitz took up the answer, and he cared to believe it was not just so that he would hold her attention again. "One would think so. However, some lords are concerned about the ramifications. There is the expense of setting up a certification program. Who would administer it? How would it be staffed? How would we ensure its quality?"

"Others are worried it will limit the economy," Talbot added. "Perhaps you've heard of Adam Smith? He wrote the theory of the *laissez-faire* economy. The more the government regulates what a businessman may or may not do, the poorer the economy will fare. It could have ripple effects all the way down to the price of bread."

"To which I argue you need healthy men to have a healthy economy."

"Enter the Diplomatic Duke." Margot smiled as she said this, glimmering at him in that teasing way of hers. Still, Fitz wondered if she meant it as an epithet.

"Forgive me," Annabelle said, "but these charlatans are surely selling false medicine because they need money, not because we have an epidemic of evil Englishmen. Wouldn't our efforts be better spent ensuring every person has food on their table?"

Fitz lifted a shoulder, not conceding the point. His attention had been called to the topic two years before when his valet died suddenly after taking a tincture procured from a so-called traveling apothecary. He had trouble conjuring sympathy for the man that sold a bottle of arsenic and claret as a cough cure. "Certainly, one hopes that if everyone's bellies were full, we wouldn't need such measures, but remember greed is one of the seven deadly sins. There will always be a man out to make a profit."

Annabelle pursed her lips, unconvinced. Margot reached for a hunk of fresh bread and dunked it straight into the stew. "Pardon my uncouthness, but I prefer to eschew London dinner manners when it comes to a rustic meal like this." Licking a stray fleck of bread from her lips, she looked to Fitz again. "Is the apothecary bill your main focus this Season?"

So distracted was he by her tongue, her lips, her bright brown eyes, that Fitz had to repeat the words to himself to understand her question. He cleared his throat. This was precisely what he had been hoping to avoid.

"No, it's just one of several."

Talbot sipped his ale. "You see, Fitz isn't content to follow the agenda set by the Prime Minister, nor by the minority party leader. He always strides into the Season with his own goals. And you never know if he's taking you to dinner to chat about something personal or to charm you into voting his way."

"If one wants to see the country progress, that's what one must do. I know I'll only succeed with one or two of my measures each year. Some will be folded into a compromise one way or another. Others will fail miserably."

Margot set down her hunk of bread. "How do you choose your agenda?"

Fitz shrugged. He'd never had to think too hard about it. Unlike Talbot, he wasn't content to simply listen to the measures proposed by others and make his vote. He'd always had strong opinions, a clear vision for what should be improved, and from there it was only a matter of aligning the proper political resources to make change happen. "I know what I want. It's a matter of timing, I suppose."

Margot's eyes dropped down to her stew. There was something in her expression that twisted Fitz's stomach; just for a moment, he thought he saw desperation. Then she popped a smile back into its place. "And just what is your vision for our country?"

All eyes at the table were on him, but he felt only hers: earnest, curious, trusting. Fitz wanted so badly to give an answer she would respect. An answer she would agree with. An answer she would love.

He cleared his throat, searching for the right words. "When I am old, I would like to take a trip across the country, and I would like to see every man and woman fitting into the puzzle. Everyone should have a role in making this world work. I don't want to see hunger or exhaustion or desperation. And I should like to have played a part in eradicating all that."

Margot let the words settle around her, then nodded, returning to her food as if he'd done no more than predict a sunny morrow.

He released his breath, realizing in all this time he hadn't yet touched the supper. It wasn't unusual for him to be so caught up in politics that he forgot his hunger or thirst, but this felt different than an ordinary dinner debate. This felt more like a baring of his soul.

Annabelle picked up the thread of conversation, asking about which lords needed to be brought into line to pass the apothecary bill. Somehow, Fitz answered, though he barely knew what he said. His attention was still on Margot and his little speech, and whether he felt better or worse for having given it.

He shook himself, disgusted. Who was this man, lost in thought – no, lost in *feeling?* Fitz did not let himself get consumed by emotions. Margot was beautiful and delightful, but nothing more. She was a fun dalliance to win a wager, not a siren to whom he'd surrender all power of thought.

Still, he lingered at the table. He and Talbot ordered jugs of ale while the ladies sipped wine, and the conversation meandered from Parliamentary measures to recent news from London to Talbot's strategy with the Duke of Surrey. "I mean to be matter-of-fact. The old man left the money specifically to Annabelle, so we are legally in the right. It's simply a question of whether the new duke contests that part of the will or not."

Fitz had interrogated them about this part of the venture on their trip north to Gretna Green. The will had assumed Annabelle would remain a lonely widow for the rest of her life; given that she had violated the spirit of it, she feared that the Duke of Surrey would decline to provide her with the sum. And Talbot was on the brink of bankruptcy. If the duke neglected Annabelle's coffers, the couple would likely have to flee to France to avoid creditors.

"The man never liked me," Annabelle said, "so *I* mean to be as silent as possible."

"And how will the Diplomatic Duke improve the situation?" Margot asked, her eyes sliding to his in a smirk.

Fitz straightened in his seat, refusing to let his thoughts be tugged by the twitch of her lips. "I'll play to his ego. Compliment his grounds, comment on how well he has taken to his title. If necessary, I'm prepared to offer to vote yes on his proposal to increase transportation sentences, though that is really a worst-case scenario."

She arched an eyebrow. "Ah, the great secret of politics. I wonder how many of our laws are decided by backroom agreements over marriage partners."

"Even more are compromises over bed partners, I daresay." Fitz didn't know why he dared say it. The air between them thickened with the suggestion of affairs. He pictured Margot in a sultry London ballroom, battled over by all the lords who would like a chance at her bed. He would strike a deal with the devil to keep anyone else from knowing the heady rush of her kisses.

Blinking, Fitz looked to the other side of the room. What rubbish. Margot was a lovely widow. She could kiss whomever she wanted. And he wasn't about to go compromising his vision – even in his imagination – to win her hand.

The conversation had moved on. Margot laughed at something Talbot said. She threw out laughs easily, low and throaty and lovely. Fitz got lost in it, and by the time he shook himself of that spell, Talbot and Annabelle were excusing themselves.

"I must say I'll miss you as a bedfellow," Annabelle teased Margot. "You smell so much nicer than dear Bernard."

"Ah, but my goodnight kisses are not nearly as sweet." Margot sparkled as she said this, earning a deep red blush from Talbot and a giggle from Annabelle.

Suddenly, Fitz and Margot were alone. She turned to him with a pixie smile. "I'm not nearly tired enough to sleep. Shall we ask the innkeeper for a deck of cards?"

He could say yes. How easy it would be. They'd play cards and flirt and drink more wine, and then he'd escort her upstairs where they each had a private bedroom. It would only take one kiss for them to decide to retire into one together. For them to tumble onto the bed. For him to discard that gray dress and unlace her corset and taste her supple body. She would be beautiful and soft in his hands. Fitz could just imagine how playful a lover she would be, nipping him here, toying with him there, before turning the raw power of want on him. A dream lover. A dream evening.

He was hard just thinking of it.

But he'd already let this go too far. Margot was only ever supposed to be a lark. A pretty widow to flirt with on his brief sojourn in the north. Fitz's thoughts today were too unruly to manage; how would they be tomorrow if he indulged in heady Margot?

Her eyes had darkened as she awaited his response, as if she could read his thoughts. She licked her lower lip. "Perhaps you prefer some other activity."

It would be so easy. But Fitz couldn't allow himself to do it. Somehow he just knew that one flirtatious word would drown him in a sea of something he couldn't handle.

He stood. The chair objected to his action and tumbled backwards. Fitz righted it, then looked back at Margot, who still wore those luminous, beautiful eyes.

He cleared his throat. "I beg your pardon, but I am too tired. Good night."

Never mind that she needed an escort upstairs. Fitz fled the room like a cowardly little boy. He didn't want to see the confusion on her face. Or feel the disappointment in himself.

January 6, 1811

Dearest Margot,

We arrived to Richmond Hall late last evening, after calming Mama's nerves for most of the afternoon. She thought you were about to hit Papa at one point, which is of course ridiculous, but you know our tempers do wear her nerves thin as muslin!

Hugh surprised me with the sweetest thing this morning. Knowing I am concerned for you, he has gone through all his newspapers from the past few months and clipped the articles having to do with weavers and Luddites and such. There are several promising dispatches about weavers peacefully petitioning magistrates for protected wages, and only a few articles about violence, so I am hopeful that you will not have a revolution on your hands.

Be safe on your journey (though likely you won't receive this until it has ended). I am grateful that you are in good company for most of it, and that His Grace will accompany you the full way. (I should like details about that in a private letter as soon as you have caught your breath!)

Sending you all my love—

Your sister,

Alice

Chapter Fourteen

It took them three more days to reach Derby. Three days cramped in Talbot's carriage, with George kicking his energy into the benches and Valentina crying every time the wheels hit a rut. Annabelle passed the time telling stories of her various adventures around Europe, pausing every now and then to touch her husband's hand or bestow a secret smile on him. Talbot rejoined with a joke here or there, but mostly kept to his little corner, an eye on the countryside passing by.

Fitz remained on his mare all three days, cantering merrily ahead of the carriage. Margot peeked beyond the curtains every so often, just to make sure he was still there. He'd been the definition of polite ever since that disastrous moment at the Crossing Lions. He solicited her opinions in conversation. He laughed at her repartees. But he hardly looked at her. He certainly didn't find himself alone with her.

Margot's cheeks burned at the memory of that night. How could she have been so forward? And so horrifyingly wrong? The moment they'd found out there were enough guest rooms that she could have her own, her mind had leapt to the notion of sneaking Fitz into it. And then the way he had stared at her when she'd suggested they play cards; she could have sworn he had wanted to kiss her – or more.

Had he refused because she'd been so bold? Or because he truly didn't want to?

Margot resolved to put it from her mind. She'd spent enough of the last three days worrying it over. Better to accept what was. Fitz was a polite friend, there to help ease her political worries. She could be grateful for that and not wish for anything else.

She was determined not to wish for anything else, in fact.

They arrived at Derby in midafternoon. Annabelle persuaded Margot to go shopping on High Street while Nurse walked the children around town. Compared to the sleepy towns they'd been passing through, Derby was a veritable metropolis: not only were there a smithy and butcher and baker, but a milliner, a cobbler, two dressmakers, and even a bookstore lined the streets, too.

They purchased items from each shop as gestures of goodwill, not that Margot needed another bolt of cotton or set of ribbons for Valentina's hair.

"How do you think it will go?" Annabelle asked, looping her arm through Margot's as they emerged from the bakery with sugared scones for the children.

Margot knew she referred to the visit tomorrow to the new Duke of Surrey. The closer they'd gotten to town, the more anxious Annabelle had grown. Her stories of French revolutionaries and Prussian riverboats had dried up. She had hunched in her carriage seat, huddling her arms across her stomach. Talbot had taken up the conversation, prattling on about racehorses just to fill the air.

Now Margot tugged Annabelle's arm playfully. "If I were the duke, I would be eternally grateful to Talbot for taking you off my hands. Can you imagine how expensive it is to pay for a dowager duchess for her lifetime? You, my lady, must cost five thousand pounds per year, and you have at least thirty years ahead of you. What a bother."

Annabelle didn't laugh, as Margot had hoped. Instead she asked earnestly, "Do you really think so?"

"Certainly." Drawing herself up in imitation of the duke's stiff-backed posture, Margot pretended to glare down through a monocle and deepened her voice. "Pay you once to be out of my hair, or put up with you for the rest of my life? Bah, do take your cheque and leave my presence at once."

At last, Annabelle cracked a smile. She placed her hand atop Margot's as they turned back towards the inn. "Tomorrow is just one day. What happens, happens."

"Precisely. This time tomorrow, you'll know your fate, one way or another. Then you can move forward." Margot dropped Annabelle's arm to lift her skirts as they crossed a puddle. "Imagine where you'll be this time next year. You'll have started your salon, I wager. Yours will already be the most coveted invitation in England."

"Or we'll have to let the house in town to pay our debts."

Margot waved this idea away. "You'll have the Prime Minister to Ambley Park for Christmas to plot the

Parliamentary agenda with him."

"Or I'll be confined at home with child, unable to do anything except stare at my swollen belly."

Margot laughed. "Of all people, you would not let a little condition such as that stop you from your mission. No, you'll be so glowing that every person wants to take your suggestions, if only to steal some of your happiness. Lo, a new bill next year to guarantee every Englishman can buy bread for his family."

As they turned into the inn's courtyard, Margot spotted Fitz at the stables. He ran a curry brush over his mare's flank, leaning close to her ear to murmur something secret.

Just a few days ago, he had murmured in Margot's ear. Now he acted as if she were any other lady.

Was it possible to be jealous of a horse?

Annabelle tugged at Margot's arm. "Let us speak in private, Margot. There's something else I must confide in you, as your friend."

Glad of the distraction, Margot took one last glance at Fitz – hoping he had seen them and now raised his eyes to catch hers – before following Annabelle upstairs to their room. Annabelle sat them at the foot of the bed, turning to take Margot's hands in her own.

"I hope you will forgive me for noting that you and Fitz have developed a certain closeness of friendship."

Margot wasn't so sure that was the truth anymore. "We have good conversation, but I am still in mourning."

"Convention is overrated. I speak from personal

experience. Observing the year of mourning for society's sake is the same torture as a cock that crows every hour to keep you from sleeping."

And yet, Margot mused, Annabelle was still bound by that convention, especially as she sallied forth to Frampton Park. If the Duke of Surrey was offended by how quickly she had thrown it to the side, her fortune was lost. One would do well to remember how far convention's grasp could reach.

"What I must confess is that earlier on our journey – before we even arrived at Bleneccle Manor – Talbot and I made a wager with Fitz. We bet that he would meet his sweetheart in these three months, and *she* would be the woman he marries, not some debutante from Almack's. Fitz took the opposite stance."

Margot smiled. It was such a foolish idea, so typical of Annabelle's warm jokes and Fitz's self-deprecation. She only wondered that there was money on the line.

"How much did you wager?"

"One hundred pounds. To be collected at his wedding."

The sum was enough to hire a whole new household staff.

"So you see, it must be in the back of Fitz's mind," Annabelle said. "I'm sure he won't let it influence him in an unsporting way, but sometimes these things hold us back unconsciously."

Fitz had said it so plainly. *I'm not looking for a bride.* What he'd meant, then, was that he could never marry *her.* He planned to win the wager, and why shouldn't he? Margot was certainly not destined to be his duchess.

Was that why he had left the room so abruptly at the Crossing Lions? Did he fear that she would force him into marriage if they went farther than a few kisses?

Did he hate the idea of marrying her that much?

Returning her attention to Annabelle, Margot squeezed her friend's hand appreciatively. "You are kind to confess to me, but I hardly expect marriage from Fitz. I'm not sure I want marriage from anyone again."

"Are you quite sure you're not upset?"

Now that the topic had been broached, Margot couldn't help but confide, "Not about the wager, no. But I do wonder if I offended him. The last two days of travel, he has hardly looked at me. I'm afraid he has tired of me."

"I can't imagine that's the case." Standing, Annabelle paced the room a few times, tapping her chin, before turning to Margot with a smile. "I have a hunch, and if you'll allow it, I believe it is time for what my friend the Comtesse de Vurennes called the *le moment d'appâter.* Rather than descend to dinner and grace Fitz with your company, as he has grown accustomed to of late, you and I shall dine privately, leaving him to stew in his fears that *he* has offended *you.*"

It was the type of game ambitious mamas batted around in ballrooms. Margot could already anticipate Fitz's shiver of distaste should he find out. Yet she preferred not to see him than to spend the evening stealing glances, hoping to find him mooning back at her.

"Let us set our own wager. I bet you five pounds that we can go the rest of the evening without speaking of a single man, with my son as the exception."

"I should hate to take the wager saying we *can't* accomplish that," Annabelle protested. "How about by the end of the evening, we will have planned what issue I will champion first?"

Shutting themselves into their bedroom, Margot and Annabelle ordered up trays of food and paper and quills. Margot spent most of the evening taking notes while Annabelle dreamed aloud of all the ways she would like to see England improve, all the people she wanted to help, all the ways she could exert influence. Annabelle's ideas were as plentiful as the stars in the sky, and they spread as wide as the blanket of night that enveloped the countryside. By the time they retired to bed, she had found herself a destiny.

Margot's head only spun as she tried to steal some of the stardust for herself.

It was a beautiful, sunny day when Margot saw them off to Frampton House. She gave Annabelle a hug for luck, then nodded at Fitz as he climbed into the carriage. He gave her a little smile, nothing like the wicked grins he had shot her before, and Margot refused to acknowledge the dart of disappointment.

She had far more important things to sort out than whether the Diplomatic Duke favored her with his attentions.

Her first stop was the wainwright, where a few carriages awaited hire. None was as luxurious as Talbot's; they had unpadded benches and wooden shutters for the windows to shut out the cold. Margot suspected their wheels would hit pockmarks harder, too, but such was her penance for refusing her father's help.

She was doing this her way, no matter if it was a trifle more uncomfortable.

She hired the largest coach, along with a driver and team of horses, to begin travel the following day. Then she got creative. At the millinery, she purchased fabric and stuffing for a pillow, then hired the junior seamstress at the dressmaker to quickly fashion some cushions for the carriage benches to better protect their derrieres.

Margot finished this last errand with a bit more spring in her step than when she had started. After all, sorting out tasks for oneself had a certain satisfaction. It may not have been perfect, but it was how *she* managed to do it, and that counted for something.

It was as she stopped into the bakery to treat herself to a snack – a cheese scone ought to do the trick – that Margot realized why she felt so free. This was her first time on her own since she'd fled to Bleneccle Manor in November.

She had been so desperate, in those dark months after Geoff's death. Everything had been overwhelming, even little Valentina's pleas for goodnight kisses. Back then, standing alone on High Street would have sent Margot into a tailspin, overthinking every move, anger and grief flooding her body, wishing more than anything that she could simply be in bed.

But now, it felt good. It felt right. Margot didn't need to hide behind her father like a little toddler scared of a shadow. She was a grown woman, a mother, a dowager countess with people counting on her.

As she licked the last crumbs of the scone from her lips, Margot had another epiphany. She was jealous of Annabelle because she had such a clear vision for her future. She coveted Fitz's easy opinions, his "I know what the change needs to be" answer. They both knew exactly what they wanted, and they had a plan to make it happen.

Margot was spending all this energy wishing she had a plan, when she didn't yet have the first part. She didn't know what she wanted.

It was time to do something about that.

From the reticule hanging at her arm, Margot withdrew her little stub of pencil and fold of paper. She had been tallying the costs of their inn stays, to better understand what kind of hospitality she owed Talbot, but there was plenty of room left on the page, so she boxed off the numbers and started a list.

What I Want to Change

There. She had a title. Now all she needed were the items to make up the list.

Margot sat back, pushing her thoughts to form something cohesive. In order to want something to change, one must first be unhappy with it, so she supposed she might as well start with what made her unhappy.

This list she didn't write down, but rather gathered in her head, each little unhappiness piling on another inside what she imagined to be a porcelain basin engraved with Geoff's face.

That Geoff had always left her in the country or with her parents or anywhere he wasn't, as if she were some sort of nuisance

That, even as his wife, she didn't have a right to know how much money Geoff had invested in the mill

That Geoff had never paid her heed when she brought up the fact that the people of Wickhamshire needed more support or more bread or more coin

That the people of Wickhamshire needed so much, and she couldn't seem to help them

That Mr. Robbins assumed her father would be the one to answer him about the militia

That her father didn't consider her able to make her own decisions

That her father never took anything she said seriously

That it had taken the protection of a man – a duke, no less – to end the argument with her father

That Fitz now seemed to be ignoring her

She would choose to avoid that last one, for now.

Interestingly, Margot noted, she wasn't unhappy any longer that Geoff had left such a mess in her lap. She resented the mess, to be sure, but not the fact that it was now her responsibility to clean it up.

She was, after all, a headstrong dowager countess. One might say she had been born for this.

Reviewing her mental list, Margot now translated that unhappiness into changes she might be able to effect. Just as Annabelle planned to improve the lot of the common man one salon at a time, Margot would plot her own initiatives.

Most of her grievances, she realized, related to the fact that as a wife and as a woman, she had no real power. So, then, she would have to focus her attention on demanding that power.

Putting her pencil to paper, Margot started listing out all the powers she wished to have:

Wives should have the right to review the family's finances

Ladies of the peer should have their own funds beyond pin money to manage the care of their parishes

A lady may be advised by men, but no man should be able to make a decision in her stead

She sat back to review the list. It hardly seemed to encompass enough. Still, if she closed her eyes and imagined a time twenty years from now, when Valentina would be marrying, Margot could almost taste the power. A wife who wasn't at the mercy of her husband. A lady who could care for her people without waiting for approval from her lord.

It was almost the stuff dreams were made of.

Opening her eyes again, Margot read through the list. It wasn't long enough, to be sure, but it was a start. After all, this was just the penciled version. When she got home to Corinium Park, she would write it out in ink, with any new ideas that came to mind. And when she was truly sure, she would embroider it into a sampler to hang in Valentina's room.

No, she corrected herself. She would embroider two samplers: one for Valentina, and one for George.

For that would be another goal: to raise her son to be a man who empowered the women around him.

Chapter Fifteen

Fitz knew it was still January, yet winter seemed to have melted away. When he'd begun this adventure with Talbot and Annabelle, even Ambley Park had been nothing but frosted fields and frozen ponds. Now, as they returned victorious to town from Frampton Park, Fitz could have sworn it was spring. The sun shone with a friendly yellow glow onto soft brown fields, and the bare tree branches swung in the easy breeze. Underneath his greatcoat, Fitz felt too warm.

Talbot and Annabelle were in fine form, now that they'd won their claim from the Duke of Surrey. It had not been so challenging, after all; Surrey had been gracious and even congratulated the couple on their marriage with a pompous speech. Fitz suspected Annabelle was too bright a light for Surrey to keep in his retinue when he had three daughters about to launch into society. It was better for everyone that she quietly retire from the Surrey family.

So that business was behind them. Fitz allowed himself a steady exhale of relief. Now he could get back to his true focus, and let Talbot revel in marriage.

At the moment, the picture of matrimony was amorous. Talbot and Annabelle hadn't let go of each other's gloved hands once since they entered the carriage, despite Fitz's presence just across the coach from them. Annabelle had kept giggling, like some silly debutante, while Talbot had kept mumbling inane things like, "I say," and, "Can you believe it?"

If this was marriage, Fitz resolved anew to avoid it, if only to keep his ability to form intelligent thoughts.

"Well, old boy, I suppose this is farewell," Talbot said, as if just now realizing that Fitz was in their company. "We do appreciate you lending a hand."

"Yes, it has been wonderful having you as a travel companion." Annabelle beamed at him. For the briefest of moments, Fitz's breath caught at being within the circle of her smile; she was a goddess lit from within. If this was the gaze she always bestowed upon Talbot, it was no wonder he had thrown his world upside down to make her his wife.

Fitz's heart widened just a bit, yearning for someone to look upon him that way. Yearning to feel so deeply that he would look upon someone that way in return.

He cleared his throat. "I am always at your service, although in this case it seems I hardly needed do anything. I daresay you are glad to be able to return to Ambley Park now."

"Indeed. Quite a bit to do." Talbot lifted an eyebrow at Annabelle, earning another of her giggles. "I hope you don't pick up any other errands while on the road to Wickhamshire so that you can return to Pembroke Abbey at last."

Fitz nodded. It was only proper that he would wish to finish up the business with Margot as quickly as possible.

He'd been gone from home far longer than planned, far longer than prudent given all his responsibilities. He shouldn't look forward to prolonging this journey, or seeing the home Margot had fixed for herself.

He should be chafing at the obligation, not dreaming of it.

"It is so gallant of you to see Lady Wickham home safely," Annabelle said. "Are you sure you'll win our wager, Fitz?"

That was enough to whip Fitz's thoughts into order. "I am merely helping a family that was gracious enough to host us."

"Of course." Annabelle looked out the window with a sigh. "It soothes my nerves knowing you'll stay on with her. I've come to consider Lady Wickham a close friend over the course of our journey. She is a splendid combination of wit and heart, don't you think?"

"Indeed." Fitz nodded with a wicked smile. "An excellent sweetheart."

Annabelle raised an eyebrow. "An accomplished lady with only good connections ahead of her."

"I'm surprised I wasn't better acquainted with her before this trip," Talbot said. "I saw Lord Wickham often enough at White's, but I hadn't met Lady Wickham until this past Season."

Annabelle murmured something about Margot being at home in confinement for much of the marriage, but Fitz's mind was caught on the specter of Wickham. Though he'd met the man a handful of times, Fitz only remembered his voting record, nothing of personality or appearance. Now his curiosity ran rampant, trying to conjure the husband who had left Margot so bewildered.

"Did he have a wit to match hers?"

Talbot's red eyebrows lifted in surprise. "He was known to give a good rejoinder. But he favored bland topics, if you ask me. He was always prattling on about investments in industry. The cotton mill, of course, but as I recall, he also had interests in a northern coal mine and one of the canal companies."

It fit with what Fitz knew of his voting record. If the bill didn't have anything to do with business, Wickham wouldn't bother to show up.

"For leisure, he preferred boxing at Gentleman Jack's to horse riding, and mostly he drifted from one card party to another," Talbot added. "No doubt too pleasure-seeking to have crossed paths with you very often."

Fitz didn't dignify that with a response either way.

"I imagine he was handsome," Annabelle sighed. "The story goes that Lady Wickham fell in love with him playing whist, and one only does that if the gentleman is handsome."

"Why do you say that so sadly?" Talbot asked. "Surely one would be happy to fall in love with a handsome gentleman."

"I certainly am," Annabelle simpered, pressing her face altogether too close to Talbot's to remain decent in

Fitz's company. When he cleared his throat, she just barely retreated. "But in Lady Wickham's case, it makes it all the more tragic that the marriage wasn't happy. To fall in love with a young, handsome man. Why, she must have thought she'd found gold when they married. But of course, life is complicated, and marriage is long. To find oneself out of love with a handsome husband is much worse than finding oneself out of love with a plain-looking one."

The carriage rumbled into the inn's courtyard as Annabelle concluded her speech. She pressed her gaze to him again. "I've said more than a good friend should. Promise me you won't let Lady Wickham come to any injury, physical or otherwise?"

This time, her face didn't glow with inner happiness. The goddess was no longer Venus but Diana: fierce and uncompromising. Her arrow was drawn, aimed for his heart if he dared trespass on Margot's goodwill.

Fitz wasn't sure how Margot would feel about her honor being protected by Lady Gresham, but it made him feel warmer for her. He placed a palm over his heart. "You have my word."

They descended to the inn, which was busy on a sunny afternoon. Fitz and Talbot retreated to the private dining room while Annabelle went to change dresses. Fitz took up a seat by the fire. He wished he had a book to read, though his mind was such a jumble he wasn't sure he would be able to focus on a page even if there were one in front of him.

Fitz had been avoiding Margot ever since the evening at the Crossing Lions. He'd spent that whole night tossing and turning, regretting his actions. He should have explained himself to her, rather than so rudely leaving. A part of him still wished he'd taken her up on the offer. Which was why he couldn't simply apologize. He didn't know why he had done what he had, only that he needed to stop being so confused.

So he'd kept his distance. He'd ridden exclusively on his mare, kept their interactions to a minimum, and hadn't indulged any of his urges to beg her forgiveness.

Now, however, they faced another two days at least in each other's company. And his head swirled with what he'd learned about Lord Wickham and with his imagination's version of a young Margot shining brightly at the man she'd beaten at whist. The grief she wore these days was heavier than a veil, muddier than pure devastation. She was confused and angry and bereft, and Fitz feared he would stir that into a deeper sludge if he kept dallying with her without knowing what he wanted.

Well, he knew what he wanted. An amusing friendship, one he wouldn't mind putting aside to return home by the end of the week. The fear was that Margot kept making him wish for more time with her.

The lady in question appeared with Annabelle in time for supper. Not having a French cook in employ, the inn did not have much imagination when it came to food, but they made up for it by serving mountains of the potatoes, roast, and carrots. Margot ordered their finest wine instead of ale in celebration of the Gresham victory at Frampton Park, which started a night-long joke of referencing the day's excursion as if it had been a battle. She was in a fine mood that evening; with a natural smile always at her lips and mischief in her eyes, she was the most chipper he'd seen her since the confrontation with Lord Eastley at Bleneccle Manor.

He had to work all the harder to stop yearning for her.

They stayed up late, the four of them, so late that when they retired, even the front room of the inn had emptied of all but the drunks, and the tired innkeeper was sweeping the floors. Fitz had a sense that the evening was magic, the kind of night that only came once in seven years with a clap of thunder, and he wanted to bottle up the feeling of good conversation, good food, and pretty women, to sip on cold winter nights when next he was alone.

They woke early to make their departures. Mr. Robbins was the first to leave, after receiving some words of instruction from Margot, as he was to arrive at Corinium Park a day ahead of them in order to alert the household for preparation.

Talbot and Annabelle left next, the lady gifting Valentina a hair ribbon and George a sweetmeat in farewell. She and Margot clung to each other's hands for a fair while, promising to write and exchanging other such notions of friendship.

It took the Wickham party a bit longer to ready for

departure. The children needed to be corralled, and then so did their things, and the carriage wheeled over from the wainwright. His mare saddled and ready to go, Fitz waited in the private dining room, sipping a weak cup of tea while skimming the Derby broadsides for news. Most of it was local scuffling – such-and-such farmer charged another with stealing his sheep – but there was one item of note: a meeting for men displaced by cotton mills to discuss alternative employment options.

Fitz wondered how many meetings of the sort were happening across the countryside, and how many had already happened in Wickhamshire.

He tucked the paper into his carrying case just as Margot ducked her head into the room. "We're finally ready to go, if you are."

She was brimming with energy again that morning. She wore her simple gray travel outfit, yet Fitz had the sensation that she emanated every color of the rainbow.

Annabelle was right in warning him off from dimming that light.

He trailed Margot to the courtyard, where both his mare and the hired carriage waited. The carriage looked respectable, if shabby compared to Talbot's. George and Valentina were already tucked into the bench beside their nurse. Margot turned to Fitz.

"Would you prefer to join us in the carriage or ride your steed?"

She was a mere two feet away from him. With a long

stride, he could close the distance between them and sweep her into another of those dizzying, delicious kisses.

He'd planned on riding Roona. She was saddled and everything. But Fitz found himself asking Margot, "Which would you prefer?"

She blinked. A flicker of unsaid words crossed her face; Fitz yearned to know what they were. Her response was a nonchalant, "I would prefer you do what you find most comfortable."

On the question of comfort, Roona was the clear winner. He had control over the speed, he wouldn't be jostled by every damn rut in the road, he breathed fresh air, and he wouldn't be pestered by children all day long. It was just as he had planned; he should ride the mare.

Yet suddenly, Fitz didn't care a whit for comfort. He had wanted a different answer from Margot, one that would tug at his heart as she pleaded for him to join her in the carriage. Well, if she wouldn't say it, he would.

He preferred to be at her side.

"I'll join you in the rig, then, if there's room."

Margot gaped at him. He'd driven the mischief from her eyes and replaced it with shock. Just when he thought perhaps his words hadn't been wise, she smiled.

Nay, she beamed.

"There's room," she said, her voice dropping to a soft velvet. "You may sit next to me."

Fitz touched the brim of his hat, then followed her into the vehicle. It was wide enough that he didn't physically touch her sitting beside her. But her dress spilled close to the hem of his greatcoat. If he put his hand down and so did she, their gloved fingertips might brush.

It was enough, for now, to keep a smile in his heart.

Chapter Sixteen

It was a wonder what a plan could do for one's spirits. Ever since Margot had written her little list, she'd felt both lighter and faster, as if she were running down a grassy hill in the freedom of summertime. Soon, she might tumble out of control, but for now, her spirits soared.

Even better, her children were behaving, and Fitz had chosen to ride with them. He more than tolerated their little party. He spent most of the morning in conversation with George, answering the thousands of questions her little four-year-old posed and entertaining him with stories of the knights of the Crusades. To be sure, he peppered in morality tales about the importance of duty, but Margot wouldn't be picky. Not today. Let the men carry on with their silly notions of duty; she chose to bask in the pleasure of Fitz favoring her family with attention again.

They rode a good sixty miles before finding an inn at dusk. It was in another small town, where the inn and tavern were accompanied only by a smithy. Margot, Nurse, and the children shared the bigger suite of rooms while Fitz graciously took the cramped quarters above the stable. There being no private dining room, only the tavern where any common man might drink, Margot was forced to take supper in her room with Nurse as her dinner companion. It was a watery leek soup with stale bread, but she was hungry enough to be grateful for any sustenance.

Margot and Nurse were more accustomed to exchanges about the children or household than supper conversation. After tucking George and Valentina into bed, they managed a pleasant meal, during which Margot learned more about Nurse's family of eight children and seventeen grandchildren and how the boys had a streak for trouble and the girls had a talent for sewing. Still, it was only a quarter to eight when they changed into their nightclothes and took their sleeping positions. Margot got the mattress while Nurse spread a tick out on the floor beneath the window.

Margot said her prayers three times, hoping to trick herself into sleepiness. She went through all the reasons she should be tired: the early breakfast at sunup, the day of travel, the food heavy in her stomach.

Yet her blood rushed through her veins with energy. Her mind kept returning to two themes—her list, and the warmth of Fitz at her side in the carriage. She wondered what he would make of her plans. Would he dismiss them as a silly woman's notions? Or as dreams too big to accomplish?

But he had seen her desires when even she couldn't. He'd understood that she needed to return to Wickhamshire, and he'd help her orchestrate it. Margot liked to imagine Fitz would read her list and smile. Perhaps even ask how he might help.

A raucous cheer rose from the tavern below, startling

Margot from her thoughts. She peeked out the window, where the stars sparkled in the sky. How much time had drifted as she indulged her ideas? Would it be another sleepless night?

Nurse choked on a snore, then turned on her side. Margot envied her the slumber. There was nothing worse than waiting for dawn to come, knowing that one couldn't sleep. Especially when one couldn't read, for fear of waking one's chamber companion, or do anything else to pass the time.

She wondered how Fitz was faring. Was he among the men cheering downstairs, or had he retired to his quarters already? She imagined him on a hay-stuffed mattress, sprawled with a book in hand, reading by the light of a stubby candle. He would strain his eyes, but somehow, Margot couldn't believe he would care.

Nurse snorted now, a guttural sound that made Margot imagine a large knot of mucus. She would never sleep, not with snores disrupting the peace.

Without thinking too hard about it, Margot rose from bed, robed herself, and crept from the room. In the adjoining bedchamber, the children slept peacefully. No one stirred when Margot pulled the door of the suite shut.

The hallway was dark, save for a wall sconce with a dying candle. Margot tiptoed away from the stairs, around the sharp corner, and down the passage that would take her to the stable room. The corridor smelled sharply of horses and manure now. Margot took a few breaths to accustom herself to the stench before going onward.

Luckily, there was only one room for her to choose as Fitz's. Warm orange light glowed through the edges of the door frame. For a brief moment, Margot hesitated; she could never take back this moment, if she went ahead and did the unwise.

He'd rejected her advances once already. She was a fool to try again.

But this was what she wanted. And Fitz was the one who told her she should do what she wanted.

Margot squared her shoulders and knocked. A fool she may have been, but at least she would know she had followed her heart.

It didn't take Fitz long to answer her knock. He wore his full travel costume, save for his greatcoat and boots. He had let his hair out of its queue, so that the blond locks hung as a loose frame to soften the sharp angles of his cheeks.

"Is anything amiss?" he asked, eyes chasing behind her as if expecting to find lecherous yeomen about to attack.

"I can't sleep." Margot heard how pathetic it sounded as soon as she said it. She took a step forward to cover for it and mustered up a response more appropriate for a mistress. "I thought perhaps you would be so kind as to entertain me."

Fitz's eyebrows rose as his eyes dropped across her body. He cleared his throat. For a moment, Margot feared he would turn her away again. But then he said – no, he *responded* in a raspy, helpless whisper, "What did you have in mind, madam?"

Locking his gray eyes with hers, she stepped close until the frills of her robe brushed against his chest. She fingered the glass button that topped his jacket, playing with it for just a second before freeing it from its hole. She trailed her fingers against his shirt as she moved downward, one button at a time. He didn't look away. She had the pleasure of watching his eyes darken with inky desire until finally she pushed the jacket from his arms.

He caught her hands in his, spun her out of the threshold and into the room, and shut the door with his foot in one elegant motion. Fitz claimed her mouth with his as he picked up where she had left off, loosening his tie, unbuttoning his breeches. She groped at his body as he freed it of clothes, sliding her palms beneath his shirt to feel the firm terrain of his chest. He took off her robe next, then lifted off her nightdress. Margot thrilled to be bare in front of him. Her skin hummed with power as Fitz savored her body, first circling her nipples with his tongue, then dipping lower. He sat her on the bed, then knelt before her, unrolling her stockings from her feet unbearably slowly. He locked eyes with her again, and Margot saw the heat of her own desire reflected back.

His touch awakened her body to so many desires she had shoved down. Margot had fooled herself into thinking she had outgrown the need for deep physical release. But now – her body was alive. Their lovemaking – if she dared call it that – pleasured her every nerve. She closed her eyes to better feel Fitz inside her. She egged him on, begging him to go harder. Just before she came, she locked gazes with him one last time. It was the look in his, one of joy, that unleashed her into an elated *petite mort*.

When she returned to her senses, Fitz had finished, too, and lay stretched beside her, a lazy grin across his lips. "Are you appropriately entertained, Lady Wickham?"

Margot pulled the haughty ennui of a lady of the *ton*. "It will do, I suppose."

He nipped at her shoulder in punishment.

Laughing, Margot rolled to her side to better face him. "You are quite kind to indulge my whims. I was afraid I'd have to stare at the ceiling all night listening to Nurse snore."

"You do me the favor, actually. I was afraid I'd have to stare at the ceiling all night listening to horses snore." Fitz skimmed a finger across her stomach. "I only regret I was stupid enough to deny us this three nights ago. We would have been so much more entertained."

Margot wanted to find out why he had fled before, but she sensed the moment was premature. She followed a different topic instead, to keep the conversation light. "It would help you win a hundred pounds, too. After all, that would have made it clear to Lord and Lady Gresham that I am the sweetheart in your little wager."

Fitz stilled. A shadow crossed his face, but Margot couldn't tell if there was anything more than dismay in it.

It was enough to make her babble. "Annabelle told

me about it, of course. I suppose she's so enraptured with Talbot she thinks everyone in the world is falling in love. Or should fall in love."

Softly, Fitz extricated his hand from hers. "I think she must be trying to tamper with the outcome if she told you about it."

Margot wasn't sure why his words nettled her, but there was something in the way he said them that made her heart stand on guard. She drew herself into as dignified a posture as she could manage while stretched naked on a narrow bed. "On the contrary, I daresay she suspects she is going to lose. She told me about it as a warning not to place too much store in your attentions."

"She speaks out of turn." Fitz snarled this; Margot had never heard such feeling in his voice, had never seen his face curl with his words.

Well, she could match it, and then some. "She spoke as my friend. You were so quick to leave the room the other night, I was sure I had offended you. Annabelle told me about the wager so that I would know I hadn't. I'm merely a passing amusement, and you were bored of me."

His eyes darkened in the candlelight, not with desire but with something deeper, uglier. "Following that logic, you must think I only fucked you tonight because you threw yourself at me?"

No one had used that word in her presence before. It wasn't polite. It wasn't kind. It was brutally honest.

Margot rolled to her feet. Not so much because she

wanted to. Her brain wasn't connected to her feet. Her brain wasn't connected to anything, at the moment. But her feet knew she needed to stand. Her hands knew she needed her robe, tugged tight as a shield.

And her mouth knew she needed to speak. "Do you deny it?"

Fitz still glared at her. "I certainly wasn't planning on seducing you tonight, if that's what you mean."

No, he'd been perfectly content in his room without her. She was the one who'd shown up wearing nothing but a nightgown. The one who'd kissed him. The one who'd pressed her unwelcome feelings against him.

Again.

Margot hadn't meant to feel anything for him. What a terrible moment to discover that she did.

"My apologies for bothering you," she spat. "I won't make the mistake again."

She wrenched open the door. She turned for one last moment, to give him a final chance to say something – anything – that would make it right.

Fitz only watched her, still and silent as a statue.

Margot squared her shoulders. She pretended she was a princess, one who lived far above the clouds and didn't need to concern herself with the esteem or lack thereof of mere dukes. There was no need to add insult to injury. There was simply good breeding. "Good night, Your Grace. I will see you on the morrow."

She couldn't resist slamming the door on her way out.

January 14, 1811

Dear Margot,

I write to you from the comfort of Ambley Park, my new home! It has been so long since I had one place to stay for any period of time, and even longer since said place was mine, that I may not venture to London at all this year, purely for the pleasure of not getting in a carriage again.

You are in our thoughts often as we reflect back on our journey, from your lovely wickedness at Bleneccle Manor to your friendship on the road. Of all the souls I have met on my travels, I count you as one of the wittiest, most loyal, and boldest women I know. (I mean that as a compliment!)

You are also in our thoughts as the whole countryside seems to be in upheaval with these Luddite troubles. You know my heart belongs to the downtrodden man, yet I pray for your safety and success as well. I recently read an article about a mob of Luddites in Stockport who attacked a gentleman's home with torches and bullets. However, I trust in your powers as a kind human who connects to fellow humans from the heart – rather than the brain or purse – to ensure that you will not be met with such treatment.

If you need us, we are but a letter and carriage ride away. (Yes, for you – and you alone – I would get back into a vehicle.)

Your friend,

Lady Annabelle Talbot, Countess of Gresham

PS Do tell me how the wager is going with Fitz!

Chapter Seventeen

Fitz felt like the plague. Physically, his head pounded from a night without sleep, and the saddle chafed against his legs as if to punish him for riding. Emotionally, he felt like a lout.

However, he assured himself it was all for the better. His relationship with Margot had, from the start, been rather like the English weather: enchanting one minute, a disaster the next, and always dictated by her moods.

The Duke of Harrodshire simply didn't have time for such capriciousness.

It wasn't as if he could marry her. There had been a moment, just after they'd made love, when Margot had been glowing, that the thought crossed his mind. Marrying her. Capturing the delightful pixie as his wife.

Then she'd brought up the wager. Margot had all but said it for him. He wouldn't marry her. He *couldn't* marry her. She was a widow, she was preoccupied, she was emotional.

Fitz hadn't meant to say such ugly things. He couldn't think what had come over him. He had barely been thinking at all. It was just that when she'd laid bare the truth – that he was *using* her, and hurting her – he hadn't liked what he'd heard.

And apparently, his only recourse had been to take it out on her.

It was all for the better. Fitz would focus on his obligation – making sure she was delivered safely to Corinium Park – and then return to Pembroke Abbey. He'd leave Margot alone, and she would disappear from his thoughts.

The turnpike was clear of both traffic and obstacles that morning, and they made good time, arriving in Wickhamshire for a late luncheon. The town was of a decent size, with three cobbled roads forming a wishbone at its heart. A fair number of people milled about, all of whom stopped and stared as the carriage and rider passed. Fitz raised his hand in greeting, noticing in particular the young men lounging idly.

Margot directed them to the tavern for a meal. She descended from the carriage with a brilliant smile—the kind that had made Fitz dream of marriage just the night before—as she reached out to take the proprietress's hand in greeting. "How good it is to be home!"

The tenor of the stares changed as the townspeople realized they beheld their countess. For the most part, Fitz sensed a positive energy. Exclamations, loud whispers sharing the news, and necks craning for a glimpse of Margot and the children filled the lane. But he also caught a few dark looks, mostly among the young men.

Margot was in the midst of introducing him to the tavern owners – Mr. and Mrs. Hainsworth – and requesting a simple luncheon. "Afterwards, I should like to make a quick tour of the town and pay my greetings to everyone before we return to Corinium Park."

The Hainsworths just about fell over themselves at the news that Fitz was a duke. Margot let them fawn over him for a few moments before saying, "Yes, well, shall we eat?"

They served the party in a dining room decorated with Wickham memorabilia. The family crest hung above the door, a letter from Lord Wickham to Mr. Hainsworth marking the birth of the latter's son was framed on the wall, and the design of the lace tablecloth even included the Wickham insignia. Fitz sat at the head, Margot to his left, and the nurse and children to his right. For one brief second, Fitz's gaze collided with Margot's. He looked away first, burning with some combination of rage and sorrow and longing he didn't care to examine.

Margot led the conversation, largely finding topics to converse about with the nurse. Fitz ate as quickly as he could to speed up the meal, though it meant Mrs. Hainsworth cleared away the soup before poor Valentina could get more than a spoonful or two. He slowed down over the roast, timing his signal to take the plates away with when the nurse had finished getting some food in the children.

"I should hate to bore you with my tour of town, Your Grace," Margot said as Mrs. Hainsworth took away the last remnants of the meal. "Perhaps you would prefer to ride ahead to Corinium Park?"

Fitz hadn't been expecting the choice. He looked at Margot now, wondering if there was a layer beneath her question he was supposed to understand. Did she want him to leave her be? Or was this a chance for him to start erasing his words from last night?

She didn't offer any hints, sitting there calmly with a blank expression on her face. Her hair had been dressed more carefully that morning, braided into a style favored by the ladies of Almack's; he hated to notice that it favored her face, highlighting her peaked eyebrows and rosy cheeks.

Fitz looked away, clearing his mind of such thoughts. He owed her an answer. Never mind what her underlying meaning might be. He was there to help her make the right decision about calling in the militia, which meant he needed to hear what the townspeople said to her.

"It would not be a bore at all, Lady Wickham. I should be pleased to join you, if I'm invited."

Her lips pursed, just slightly. "Certainly."

So they set out as one party, little Wharton holding Margot's hand while the nurse carried Valentina behind them. Fitz supposed Margot included the children as part of her goodwill campaign; the local matrons would bestow more favor upon a little lord with irresistible ringlets than on an absent family.

They stopped in to visit the baker, the blacksmith, the wainwright, the soapmaker, the bookseller, the butcher. Margot knew them each by name, which shouldn't have surprised Fitz but did. She remembered their family members, too, and knew who had come into some money or moved to London. Moreover, she had the right words for whatever news they shared now. She congratulated the baker, whose wife had just borne their eighth child. She nodded along with the blacksmith as he decried the youth who threw pebbles at his door in their spare time. And she cried with the soapmaker upon hearing that his son had been killed at the Battle of Bussaco.

Fitz watched it all from afar, not wanting to insert himself where he wasn't needed. He'd embarked on the tour expecting that Margot would need his assistance in sorting out appropriate recompenses for complaints, but he'd underestimated her. At Bleneccle Manor, she'd been so happy not to return to Wickhamshire that Fitz had supposed she'd spent her five years as countess locked up in Corinium Park, planning dinner parties and berating her husband for leaving her in the country while he ran off to London.

Now he realized how he had misjudged her. He didn't know why she had fled Wickhamshire, but it was clear she hadn't frittered away her responsibilities. If anything, she'd taken them more seriously than the average lady of the realm.

Surprising him again, Margot broke their silence as they walked back to collect the carriage from the tavern. "What do you think of Wickhamshire?"

She asked it with another blank expression, except her eyebrows drew together just a bit, as if to shield herself from his response.

Fitz hated to think she needed shielding from *him*. Oh, he knew he'd hurt her the night before, but now he couldn't even remember why. What had been so offensive to him that he had needed to push her away so? To send her running back to her bedroom without even tying her robe shut?

Margot was a beautiful, intelligent, emotional woman. She had only been pointing out the truth, which was that he was using her for a wager. And instead of admitting that things had changed, that the wager was far from his mind, that he wanted only to keep her in his arms for as long as he possibly could, Fitz had turned into a monster. Said ugly things. Hurt her even more.

He was a lout. And a fool.

It was time to admit it, if only to himself. He was in love with this dowager countess, who cared for her people and yearned for something more and let herself feel whatever mood crossed her heart.

"I should hope you don't hate it so much that you feel the need to stay silent," Margot prodded, returning Fitz to the moment and to her question.

He bowed his head, the best apology he could muster at the moment. "I don't hate it at all. Of course, I've only had a sampling, but so far, I find the town quite charming. In fact, I daresay I love it."

Margot frowned. His words were surprising, he supposed, but having said them, he didn't care. In fact, Fitz found himself grinning like a fool. Soon enough, he would prove to her he meant it.

Chapter Eighteen

Margot didn't know what to make of the charming Fitz who squinted through the sun at her with a smile. Just an hour ago at luncheon, he had barely uttered a word, refused to look at her, oozed hatred from his every sigh. Now he was practically spouting poetry to confess his love for her town.

Better to ignore it. She had enough on her mind without adding to it deciphering the Duke of Harrodshire. Her thoughts raced from catching up with so many parishioners. She needed to remember to send a gift to Mr. Vickers to mark the birth of his daughter and something to the Wyes to commemorate their son. Moreover, the smithy and the butcher shop shared a wall that was dangerously sagging inwards, and Margot could only imagine they hadn't fixed it for lack of funds, so she needed to provide a solution before both buildings caved in.

And on top of all that, from the way George was whinging about walking too fast, she estimated they had five minutes before he melted into a tantrum, which absolutely wouldn't do with every eye in town watching them.

The only option was to speed up, the faster to get to the carriage, but that only made George whinge even louder.

"You are ever so good at walking, Wharton," Fitz said.

"Why, when I was your age, I could barely walk for ten minutes, but you've been on your feet for an hour already. You've almost passed the test, you know."

Margot decided against peering at Fitz, though she desperately wanted to. She wanted to see whether his lips twitched at whatever game he was playing, or if his blond eyebrows were peaked in the way that tempted her to kiss him, or if he was pulling the blank, stoic expression he'd worn all morning.

She wouldn't look, though. She didn't care what he was trying to do. She had her children and her people to worry about. There was no room in her mind or heart for a duke.

"What test?" George asked.

"Why, the test to become a Knight of the Round Table, of course."

Margot did not care to notice that Fitz had very cleverly stopped George's whimpering.

"The first test is to take a long journey. The second is to walk without complaint for a thousand steps. Can you count to a thousand?"

George shook his head.

"That's all right. I reckon you've taken nine hundred and ninety steps. That means we only need to count ten more for you to pass the test. One, two..."

Now George joined in the counting, and even Valentina squawked "four" from Nurse's arms. Very well, Fitz was charming. This was not new information. Margot shook her head to better remember what happened *after* his charm wore off.

"One thousand! Am I a knight now?"

"Ah, there's still another test to pass."

Of course there was. One had to earn Fitz's esteem with tests one didn't even know about. Margot swallowed hard against a lump in her throat, but emotion still prickled her eyes. She refused to replay the scene again, since it was all she'd done in the carriage that morning. She'd concluded two things: she shouldn't have brought up the wager, and she didn't know why that had triggered him to push her away.

Reaching the courtyard, she said, "That's enough now," though she'd lost track of what tale Fitz was telling George. "George, take Nurse's hand and climb into the carriage like a good boy. You and Valentina are going to take your naps at home, at Corinium Park. Isn't that exciting?"

"What about His Grace?" George asked. "Is he coming with us?"

Never mind *her*. George didn't have a care in the world when it came to his mother, but God forbid precious Fitz leave him alone.

Margot smoothed the thought out of her mind. It was only natural George would ask after Fitz, his new favorite playmate. She wouldn't take her anger out on her son when it was a grown man who had so enraged her.

She turned to the man in question, looking carefully at his ear rather than anywhere dangerous like his eyes or his mouth. "What say you, Your Grace? Would you like to head to Corinium Park or accompany me to the mill?"

"I'll accompany you to the mill." Fitz turned to George. "A knight never knows whether he is being tested or not. If you are on your best behavior, you just might pass the third test before I return."

George stood slack-jawed as he considered this possibility. Nurse hustled him up the carriage steps. Margot almost climbed in with them. The last thing she wanted was to be alone with Fitz. But she had responsibilities to face, and she wasn't interested in running away from them again.

Mr. Hainsworth drove them to the mill in the inn's wagon. The back was littered with dirt and scraps from the food and barrels it usually carried, so all three of them squeezed onto the driver's bench behind the team of two horses. Fitz sat in the middle, between Hainsworth and Margot, which meant she had to scoot precariously near the edge of the bench to avoid touching him.

"You've got a powerful seat as keeper of the tavern, Mr. Hainsworth," Fitz said as the horses plodded down the road between frozen fields. "I wonder, what would you say the mood of the town is like?"

Mr. Hainsworth straightened at the compliment. "I suppose it's a fine mood, Your Grace. We sure are glad to have Lady Wickham and the little lord back in town. If I may say, my lady, you are a sight for sore eyes."

Margot smiled at Hainsworth, catching the look Fitz

gave her as she did so. She couldn't quite tell if his eyebrow raise was an "I told you so" or simply an appreciation that she had received a positive welcome. It didn't matter either way, of course.

"We are glad to be home," Margot said. "It is always a pleasure to see you and Mrs. Hainsworth in particular. You are gracious hosts."

The innkeeper blushed, a charming sight on a man in his sixties.

Fitz let the silence settle for a few moments before trying again. "I was impressed with our tour of the town. Wickhamshire is quite industrious compared to some of the other villages I have seen. Has the mill been good for business?"

Mr. Hainsworth flicked his tongue across his teeth before answering. "After a long shift, the men like to relax with a pint, you see, before going home, so I suppose it's been good for me. Not so sure it's been good for the Vickers or Wyes or Crokers."

The wagon rumbled over a frozen rut in the road, heaving them all with a good bump. Suddenly, Margot was in the air, and her stomach dropped as she realized she might not land back inside the wagon.

But before she could so much as shriek, a strong arm hooked around her waist and hauled her safely onto the wagon bench. Fitz's gray eyes looked true with alarm when he asked, "Are you quite all right, Lady Wickham?"

Margot's heart pounded, and not just because of the

near accident. She forced herself to look to the road ahead rather than get lost in his crystal irises. "Yes, thank you, Your Grace."

"If you don't mind the impropriety, I think it might be prudent to keep my arm around you until we reach the mill."

Mr. Hainsworth hmmed in agreement. "My apologies, Lady Wickham, but I think His Grace is correct."

Margot didn't need two men to tell her that she was in danger of falling off a wagon. She nearly demanded Fitz remove his arm simply to disprove them. But being right wasn't worth a broken limb; not in this instance, anyway.

She answered Fitz with a prim nod, still refusing to look at him. He took no liberties beyond keeping his arm firmly around her waist, yet that was enough to drive her to distraction. She was practically in his lap, inhaling his ducal cologne, feeling the strength that ran from his fingertips to his core. Her body reacted instinctively, loosening and warming in places she'd rather not admit to. This was a safety measure, and that was it.

To distract herself, Margot forced her thoughts back to the visits in town and how they related to her list. The only women she'd visited with were Mrs. Hainsworth and Mrs. Wye, the latter of whom had walked over from her cottage to tearfully accept condolences for the loss of her son. Should she have tried harder to seek out the women of the village? Or should she be focusing on how to make the women more visible in the first place?

The wagon jostled again, and Margot landed more firmly against Fitz's chest. She leaned away, so as not to revisit the firmness of his body. He had no right to be so attractive when he could so easily push her away.

Thankfully, the mill was now in sight, rising like a pimple on the face of the muddy plain. Black smoke billowed from its chimney like a witch's curse from her cauldron. How Margot wished Geoff had never built the thing.

No matter. She would find a way to make everything right.

Mr. Hainsworth hitched the wagon beside the mill's carts, which were in the midst of being loaded with the day's bolts of muslin. "I'll be right here to take you back to Corinium Park whenever you are done."

Margot jumped to the ground as gracefully as she could manage, then turned and offered Fitz her hand to help him descend. He grinned. "How gallant, Lady Wickham."

She did not return his smile.

The mill foreman, a Mr. Nickerson, had been notified of their arrival and rushed forward to greet them. He was a thin man, with a shabby suit and a brown moustache that drooped over his front lip. He bowed from the waist. "Your Grace, Lady Wickham, you honor us with your presence."

"Thank you for allowing us to disturb you," Margot said. "I realize it is short notice, but as I have been gone so long, I am anxious to hear how the mill is doing, and His Grace is eager for a tour."

"Not a disturbance at all." Mr. Nickerson led them inside the mill. Margot had toured it once before, when it had first opened, but she mostly remembered how Geoff had leapt from one machine to another, exclaiming over what each could do. Now she put herself to the task of listening to the details. The clacking spinning mules produced 240 miles of cotton thread per day, which then went into the fearsome looms to transform into bolts of muslin, all powered by water from the river meandering through Wickham.

She asked more questions, too. "When do the workers report to the factory each morning?"

"Their workday is from seven in the morning until seven at night," Mr. Nickerson answered. It was her question, yet he directed his answer towards Fitz. "They are hard workers from these parts, Your Grace."

"I should say," Fitz agreed congenially.

"Do they work that whole time?" Margot pressed. "Surely that is too long for any one person to be at a task."

"They have thirty minutes for lunch at midday." Again, Mr. Nickerson looked at Fitz as he responded.

"Where do they eat?" Margot had seen the whole of the building by now and there hadn't been a single dining table.

"They eat outside." Again, all his comments were directed to Fitz, as if his gaze were glued to the duke's form.

She had resolved to find ways to empower women,

so she might as well start now. "You may speak directly to me, Mr. Nickerson. I am the one asking the questions, and I might remind you that I am your patroness, not His Grace."

Already, just saying the words, Margot felt taller. Mr. Nickerson's jaw flapped open, then shut again.

"Furthermore, eating outside during winter is not conducive to one's health. I challenge you to find a better solution before my next tour."

Mr. Nickerson looked to Fitz, as if asking whether she was to be believed or not. Margot walked ahead, biting her tongue instead of biting the man's head off. She must be patient as she mussed feathers, lest she roust the birds from the nest entirely.

"I am a mere tourist," Fitz said. "However, I am curious about how the townspeople have welcomed the mill. Any concern of Luddites about?"

Mr. Nickerson's tone darkened. "Aye. They broke into the mill down in Billings-on-Lewen not one week ago, smashed the looms to pieces. I've taken to sleeping in my office, in case they try anything here."

Margot turned to face the men. "Surely that's too dangerous, Mr. Nickerson. What if they should attack you, instead of the looms?"

"I keep my hunting gun with me for just that reason." The man looked her straight in the face, now. "If I may, my lady, your worries would be better spent on preparing for a riot than coddling the workers. They're earning an honest wage, and that's enough for them. It's the ruffians that should concern you."

The hair on her arms stood on end, though she couldn't say if she was afraid of the riot Mr. Nickerson predicted or the fierce, angry gleam in his eyes.

Either way, she wasn't about to let him, or Fitz, see that she was frightened. She aimed for the old standby *ton* expression of boredom. "Thank you for the advice."

They returned to the mill yard. The carts of cotton had left, so that only a few tied horses remained beside Mr. Hainsworth, who napped beneath the protection of his hat.

"I appreciate your time, Mr. Nickerson," Margot said, striving for a friendlier tone now. "The mill was particularly important to my husband and continues to be important to me. I expect I shall be dropping in regularly to see how you are faring."

If possible, the man's moustache drooped even lower. "I write regular reports to Mr. Robbins, my lady."

"Even so. One understands so much more when one sees it in person." Margot was just about to release the man from his misery when she saw three other men from the corner of her eye. They approached from the road with long strides. Red mud splashed onto their breeches from the energy of their steps. Margot had just recognized the one in the middle as Josiah Beauford – a broad weaver – when he launched a wad of spit directly at her skirts.

"A pox on the Wickham family for bringing this abomination to Wickhamshire."

For a moment, all she could do was blink. She'd visited Josiah and his wife Millie often, at first because their oldest child was sickly but then because they were among her favorite tenants. They had a sense of humor about life that inspired Margot.

She supposed she had been naïve to think any bond would protect her from their ire.

Her second of surprise ended when, beside her, Mr. Nickerson started to react. From the corner of her eye, she saw him lunging forward, fingers folding into a fist.

Margot held her arm out to stop him. "That will not be necessary, Mr. Nickerson. They have done me no harm."

It took Fitz's hand on Nickerson's shoulder to stop the man once and for all. Meanwhile, Josiah and his friends glared Margot down. "You've done us harm, though. The Wickham name is nothing so long as this mill is open."

"I have been gone too long, Mr. Beauford. However, I have returned, and I mean to do right by all of Wickhamshire."

Josiah glowered for a moment longer. Then he spit again – this time into the mud at his side – and turned on his heel.

Margot didn't breathe until the men had retreated all the way out of the yard. Then she exhaled, alarmed to hear her own breath shake in the air.

"I'd have those men arrested, if I were you," Mr. Nickerson growled.

She didn't have a response to that, save that she

would not do it. "It's time for us to return to Corinium Park."

It was only when she reached the wagon that Margot dared look at Fitz. His jaw was tight, his nostrils flaring. She wondered how he would have handled the scene had they been his tenants. Would he have punched them? Arrested them?

She was glad he had followed her lead here. Whatever his reaction would have been, he'd trusted her to manage the men as she saw best.

He climbed into the wagon, then helped her up. This time, he didn't ask her permission to secure her at his side with his arm. And this time, she didn't mind being held, for her body had started to tremble.

Chapter Nineteen

By the time they reached Corinium Park, Fitz had settled down to a civilized state. His heart no longer thundered louder than the cantering hooves of the horses; his fists no longer curled reflexively as he thought of those men leering over Margot.

How Fitz had wanted to pummel them. He'd sensed danger as soon as they appeared on the road, and when they'd spit at her skirts, it had taken every ounce of control not to tackle them then and there.

But Margot had handled it beautifully. The men had been looking to get a rise out of her, yet she had called their bluff, leaving them no option except to retreat. Fitz's reaction would have escalated the whole situation into grounds for a riot. Margot's had diffused it.

Now she leaned into him as he held her within the wagon. For a moment, she even rested her cheek against his shoulder. So she wasn't made of steel, then. She trembled with fear like a sensible creature; she was simply brave enough to know when to show it.

He was glad she accepted his arm this time. Margot had been cool and distant on the wagon ride from town to the mill, which Fitz could of course understand. He'd been a brute to her not twenty-four hours ago. As much as he wished a few well-placed smiles and flirtations might smooth things over, he owed her an apology. In private. And then all he could do was hope she would be kind enough to forgive him.

It only took a quarter of an hour to reach Corinium Park from the mill. The park surrounding the home was much like any other country estate Fitz had visited. Yawning green lawns, a yew-hedged garden, a Grecian folly standing proud and useless atop the hill. The house itself was rather understated, a simple rectangle with a limestone façade that put one in mind of a lemon cake. Its only architectural ornamentations were two Ionic columns framing the front door. If one were to place it next to other great houses, it would look rather like a shabby cottage.

Fitz approved. He found expenditure on projects such as painting window casings with gold leaf – as his Cavendish relatives had - to be an extravagant waste of money.

A footman was awaiting them by the time Mr. Hainsworth pulled the wagon around to the door and helped Margot down from the carriage. Fitz felt suddenly cold without her body beside him. With the eyes of the household on him, he clasped his hands patiently behind his back and kept a polite distance from their mistress. She had pressed on a smile again, first thanking Mr. Hainsworth for the ride and then greeting the footman. She even asked after the footman's sister's gout.

One wouldn't have known she had been physically threatened within the past hour, if one hadn't been standing next to her when it happened.

The housekeeper, having been forewarned of their arrival, had Fitz escorted directly to his rooms. He hesitated before following, looking to Margot, but she had already changed the direction of her attention.

She didn't need any more of his comforting, then.

He was given the suite of honor, situated at the front of the house with two sets of windows, which meant he had a view of the park both to the north and to the west. The rooms were tastefully decorated, with Brussels carpets under his feet, elegant furniture, and wallpaper that didn't distract yet added cheer. Best of all, the bedroom featured a small set of shelves that boasted a full set of *The History of the Decline and Fall of the Roman Empire.*

But Fitz was, for once, in no mood to read. He had too much to think through. There was the quandary of Wickhamshire. Given the obvious unrest, should he advise Margot to call in the militia, just in case?

And then there was Margot. Would she accept his apology? And if she did, then what? Could they possibly be special friends, or was he doomed to know her only as an acquaintance?

Would he be satisfied without any further arrangements between them?

Fitz rang for a bath. The best way to tidy the mind was to tidy one's surroundings, and that included tending to a body that hadn't been properly cleaned or shaved since they'd departed from Bleneccle Manor. The hot water felt luxurious, soothing his muscles as it washed away the dirt clinging to him from the road.

It calmed him, too. On the question of Margot, he didn't need an answer in order to apologize. He owed it to her no matter what came next. Moreover, neither of them could expect much more than a special friendship. She was, after all, a widow of only seven months, and mother to an heir, to boot. To marry would not only raise eyebrows, it would complicate Margot's property holdings in the extreme. When Fitz married, he would need a duchess without past entanglements or children, one who could focus all her energy on his many holdings.

So he would apologize, and he wouldn't worry about what came afterwards.

Shaved, clean, and wearing his evening suit for a change, Fitz felt like a new man. He was about to descend for dinner when a footman arrived carrying a tray. "Lady Wickham said to set this out for you here, Your Grace. She is eating with the children tonight and didn't want you to be alone in the dining room."

Fitz wondered if that were the true reason, or if Margot simply didn't want to see him. Well, she didn't know he had spent so much time plotting an apology. Given what he'd said the night before, she might even assume he would prefer not to dine with her.

He gave her precisely one hour to continue in that line of thinking. Then, once he estimated she would have finished with the children, Fitz ventured downstairs. He poked his head into two drawing rooms, a portrait gallery, and a library before finally finding Margot in the study.

She sat behind the wooden desk, sifting through papers, her eyebrows drawn, the picture of calm concentration. The soft hues of dusk mixed with firelight to color everything in pinks and oranges. For a moment, Fitz allowed himself to simply observe Margot, to wallow in the beauty of a woman at work.

Then he cleared his throat. "Do you mind if I intrude?"

Her first reaction was the truest—surprise mingled with pleasure. Then she looked back down at the papers. "Not at all. Did you enjoy your dinner? Cook was quite chuffed to be serving a guest after all this time with no one at home."

"Please pay him my compliments. It was delicious." Shutting the door behind him, Fitz moved to the leather chair opposite the desk, but he didn't sit. It didn't feel right quite yet.

The moment stretched too long, and Margot peeked up at him again. "Did you want to discuss something?"

He inhaled deeply to bolster himself. He'd never had to do this before. "I owe you an apology. I said terrible things last night."

Margot offered a fleeting smile. "I think we can agree neither of us was on our best behavior."

Her words were a gracious feint; Fitz could see in the way she avoided his gaze that she didn't mean them. "I beg to differ. There was no equality in our argument. You only spoke the truth. What I said…"

"Was also the truth." Margot rose, her eyes meeting his with a solemn calm. "I threw myself at you after a few kisses here and there. I'm no innocent. I should know better than to do so and expect anything. And I don't expect anything. I really do find the wager quite amusing, and now that the Talbots are secure in their fortune, I rejoice in you winning their money. Please, let's put it all behind us."

She held out her hand, as if they could shake on such a thing.

Fitz ignored it. That same overwhelming feeling of…feelings was overcoming him, just as it had the night before. This time, however, he meant to use it productively instead of turning into some sort of monster.

"You believe I'm using you as some kind of pawn, all in the name of a hundred pounds. I'm not. When we first met, yes, I thought you would be the perfect dalliance to win. But Margot, there is nothing about the wager in how I feel about you." He stepped around the desk, taking her two hands in his now. "You are enchanting. You've cast your northern spell on me. So much so that I *had* to avoid you, you see, because I was frightened. I've never been in love before. And I'm afraid I've been in love with you since you first insulted me at dinner."

Margot let out a little breath. Fitz landed a finger on her lips before she could say anything.

"I don't deserve your love in return. Not yet. Not after how I treated you last night, or even before that, at the

Crossing Lions. But perhaps you'll allow me to stay and prove myself to you. I don't know what the future could hold for us, but I should hate to say goodbye to you now."

She caught his finger in her palm and pulled it away to smile. "Would you think it terribly wanton of me to kiss you right now?"

There was only one response to that. Fitz swept her into his arms and touched his lips to hers. He wanted his kiss to be a sonnet, a delicate outpouring of the love that filled him, but it quickly turned into a limerick as their bodies remembered the night before. Fitz spilled her onto the desk and across the papers, almost overturning the pot of ink as he dotted kisses down her jaw and neck down to the outline of her bosom straining against her neckline.

When Margot let out a throaty moan of pleasure, Fitz lifted her skirts to see if he could earn more of those. He started with his finger, watching her eyes darken as he circled her wet nub, then descended to lick her to a frenzy. He would get drunk on her, if he wasn't careful. But he couldn't bring himself to care, especially not when she writhed and whispered and moaned and finally shook with the power of a deep orgasm.

He stood again, freeing himself of his trousers while Margot smiled in a daze. She reached out to stroke him, but he didn't let her pursue that for too long. He was too hard, too ready for her. "I want to be inside you," he whispered instead, nipping her earlobe as he did, and he thrilled in how she shivered in pleasure.

"Oh, yes please," she breathed, which was all the inducement Fitz needed to brace her against the desk and enter.

The act was no different than any other time he'd done it. She was wet and hot and his whole body hummed inside her. The desk creaked noisily in chorus with their thrusts. Fitz's palms found her ass and his lips found her neck and breasts and lips and then he was in sweet release, gasping at the pleasure that erased all thought.

It was no different, and yet he felt as he never had before. For it was Margot who was wrapping her arms around him as he returned to himself, Margot who grinned wickedly as they put their clothes to rights, who teased him with a mischievous glance as he wiped himself clean. It was Margot, and he loved her, and she knew he loved her.

Fitz didn't suppose he'd ever been happier.

The study had darkened with the setting sun when Fitz finally came to his senses. Restoring their clothes, they nestled together on Margot's chair, she on his lap. His gaze landed on the desk, and he smiled ruefully. "I hope you'll let me put those papers to rights for you. They're looking awfully crumpled and creased now."

She heaved a sigh as she followed his gaze. "No matter what they look like. They still tell the same terrible story."

"And what is that?"

Margot lifted a sheaf of them as evidence. "The mill. It is obvious to me why the townsfolk aren't happy with the mill. The work is long and hard, and away from home, to boot. Yet even if I push Mr. Nickerson to make improvements, the weavers will still be without income, and they're the ones who seem to be making trouble. On top of it all, I can see now much of our family's income is dependent on the mill."

Fitz tightened his arms around her. "You recognized the men in the yard today. Do you think they meant real harm?"

A shadow crossed her face at the reminder of the episode. "They weren't going to hit me, if that's what you mean. But their anger was true."

Anger. How Fitz wished the emotion would stop getting in the middle of things.

"Do you think I should have had them arrested?" Margot's voice was soft as she asked this, betraying her self-doubt.

Fitz resisted the urge to squash her insecurities with a good, firm kiss. "I thought you handled it magnificently. Far better than I could have."

She pinkened at this. Then she lifted her great round eyes to him again. "Do you think I should request the militia?"

"First of all," he stalled, "as Lord Lieutenant, you wouldn't be requesting it. You would be ordering it, within all your rights."

Margot raised an eyebrow. "Should I issue orders to the militia, then?"

It was the question of the week, yet Fitz still didn't

have a response. He'd known all along it wasn't his to answer. For the first time, however, he believed Margot might make a better decision than he would, anyhow.

"I don't know," he admitted. "What do you think?"

Margot pursed her lips. Fitz sensed a thoughtful answer coming, one born of a week's worth of turning the problem over in her mind. Before he could hear it, however, they were interrupted by hoofbeats on the gravel drive.

Lifting Margot from his lap, Fitz crossed to peer out the window behind her desk. A lone rider came to a stop at the front of the house. It was only as he swung a heavy leg over the saddle to disembark that Fitz recognized none other than Lord Eastley.

"How curious," he breathed. "It's your father."

"Papa?" Catching a glimpse of Lord Eastley through the window, she went to the study door and called out to the butler, instructing him to show her father to the green drawing room. Her fingers pulled nervously at her skirts. Fitz wanted to calm her, but he settled for following her down the corridor to a drawing room overlooking the back gardens. By the time her father was announced, Margot had mustered up a smile.

With a week's worth of travel on him, Lord Eastley looked worn and tired compared to the vibrant host Fitz had grown accustomed to at Bleneccle Manor. His steps were slower, his demeanor less sure.

"Papa, we weren't expecting you," Margot said, moving forward as if to hug him. In the end, she only clasped his hands.

"Our parting was in anger. I wanted to clear that up before it simmered for too long." Noticing Fitz for the first time, Lord Eastley released Margot's hands and bowed. "Your Grace, thank you for escorting my daughter here safely."

Fitz could only see the back of Margot – the bristle of her shoulders, the angle of her neck, the clench of her elbows – but he could feel the electricity in the room, and he knew it was not meant for him. He opened his mouth to excuse himself.

Only instead of words ringing through the air, a crack – like a shot – tore through the room, followed by the terrible crash of a windowpane shattering. A rock landed two feet from Fitz; glass fell on his shoulders, prickled his skin.

In shock, he turned. A pack of men advanced from a hundred yards away, tearing across the back lawn like thieves, thick flames rising from torches in their hands. One in front raised his arm, and another rock sailed through where the drawing room window used to be, this time whizzing past Fitz and landing dangerously close to Margot.

She stared at the rock for only a second. Next, her eyes found Fitz's, and he saw in them more than he could offer: a clear understanding, a fearless response. His every instinct said to scoop her into his arms and tuck her away somewhere safe, somewhere pretty. But instead, he waited for her to square her shoulders, and then he followed.

Chapter Twenty

Corinium Park was under attack. Her children were asleep upstairs, and their house was under attack.

Margot only had one option. She had to stop this before the men set the place on fire.

Stop this before it got so ugly there was no point of return.

She allowed herself one deep inhale to gulp in her panic. Then, with the exhale, she marched towards the garden.

Her father grabbed her arm, pulling her backwards. "What are you doing?"

Margot didn't know why her father had decided to follow her to Wickhamshire. Her first reaction upon seeing him had been a flood of relief, but she didn't have time now to parse her feelings or justify her actions. She yanked herself free of his grasp. "Let me handle this."

"They'll kill you, or worse!" He reached for her again, two hands aiming to lock her down. Fitz stepped between them, facing Margot.

"With your permission, Lady Wickham, Lord Eastley and I will arm the male servants, in case you need defense. We will await your order."

Earlier – had it just been a few minutes ago? – Fitz had called her Lord Lieutenant. This must be what that meant. Corinium Park was her castle, and she its lord.

Margot didn't intend to make the same mistakes the knights of old had. She had no interest in being trapped in a cycle of violence.

But her children were still upstairs, and the men were still throwing rocks against her walls.

"Fine. Make sure there are guards at the nursery."

Margot resumed her journey to the garden door. The men had slowed their run as they approached the house, a signal to her that they didn't truly want to attack a widow and her children. This was the next move in their chess game, not a full-out assault.

At least, she hoped that was the case.

Stepping out onto the marble deck, Margot nearly lost her courage. Now she could see the group better. She had thought there were four or five men; now she counted twenty to thirty, snarls of hatred on all their faces.

All the more reason to get this in hand as soon as possible. Margot spread her arms wide in a gesture of peace. She prayed to keep the fear from her voice as she projected, "Good evening. Won't you come in for tea?"

The men were close enough now that she could smell the oil of their torches. Josiah Beauford led the group, a rock still clenched in his strong fist. She recognized some of the other men too, all weavers whose cottages she had visited to tend the sick or celebrate a birth or share a Christmas gift.

None of that was enough, not if you took away a man's

livelihood.

"No mill or no Wickhams!" Josiah shouted. He needn't have screamed – Margot could hear him just fine as he trampled her flower beds – but she supposed he was saying it for his men just as much as for her. "Shut down the mill!"

The rest of the group took up the chant. "No mill or no Wickhams! No mill or no Wickhams!"

Behind her, Margot could hear her father roar, "She doesn't know what she is doing, damn it!"

She had no time for her father's doubts, not now. Margot fixed her attention on Josiah, who loved his Millie and his children and only feared that they'd end up in the parish poor house. She knew the desperate suck of fear. She had felt it for months since Geoff had died, had only just escaped its dangerous spiral. She wouldn't let it rule her now.

With the men still chanting, Margot descended the stairs to meet them on the gravel path, knees shaking with every step. Josiah backed away when she landed only a foot away from him. For the briefest of moments, the snarl disappeared from his face.

"I should like to discuss this with you," Margot said, directing her words to Josiah but making sure to include all the men in her gaze. "Won't you come inside, and we can sort out what is to be done?"

Josiah glanced to another man – Isaac Tilkes – and Margot noted him as a second leader to win over. In his fifties, Isaac was a bachelor who lived alone with his mother, but he had trained most of the weavers as his apprentices. He was, perhaps, more powerful than Josiah in swaying the group.

"At the very least, I should like to give you my very late Christmas gifts," Margot pressed. "I have a bar of special northern goat milk soap that I promised your mother, Mr. Tilkes."

That earned her a grimace, but it also brought on a nod from Isaac. Josiah lifted his hand in the air and cut off the chant. "Put out your torches!"

Margot noted he didn't direct the men to disarm, and in fact tucked his own rock into his pocket. Well, she would have to rely on good conversation to keep them from using any weapons within her house.

She led the men up the stairs and through the French doors. Her butler, Yarwood, waited, a pistol in his hand. That set Margot's heartbeat racing. She dared herself not to let it show. "We will have tea in the blue drawing room."

Fitz and her father stood tense, waiting. They, too, had guns. Fitz had Geoff's walnut dueling pistol tucked into his belt, while her father carried the hunting rifle.

"If you put away your firearms, you may join us for tea," Margot told them. She focused on continuing her walk as serenely as possible while her father sputtered. Turning as a good hostess, she offered Josiah and Isaac an apologetic smile. "We won't have chairs for everyone, I'm afraid, but we should all be able to fit."

The only sound was two dozen pairs of boots padding

down her carpeted hall. Margot entered the drawing room first. It was her lesser-used drawing room, as it was too large for the average social call. She had intended to employ it as a ballroom, though Geoff never had let her plan a house party. Well, it was perfect for fitting nearly thirty men in one space to sort out the mess.

Margot sat in the Chippendale chair opposite the fireplace, leaving the settee and two other chairs for the men to fight over. Her father and Fitz stood behind her, which made Margot feel both safe and dwarfed at the same time.

While Josiah, Isaac, and three other weavers sat, one of the maids brought in the tea service. Margot unlocked the tea chest and evaluated how much she would need to blend to serve two dozen men.

Half her tea supply, at least. It wouldn't do to serve only a few of the men, however; not when the issue at hand was the group's ill-treatment. If peace cost her a months' worth of tea, it was well worth it.

"It will take some time to prepare tea for everyone," Margot said, heaping generous scoops of green and black tea leaves into her mixing bowl, then transferring them to the teapot. "In the meantime, gentlemen, let's begin. I must apologize first that I have been tardy in learning about the late Lord Wickham's accounts, so I am just now learning of your situation. I should like to hear from you directly what your grievances are."

She caught another glance between Josiah and Isaac as she set another teapot to brew. Then Josiah cleared his throat. "It's not too complicated, my lady. Weaving is a family craft, one that takes years to learn and should pay well. The mill uses steam looms, which go faster but don't do the job as well. If my daughter walked out wearing cotton woven at the mill…I'd be ashamed, that's to say the least. The steam loom doesn't take as much training, see, so they don't pay a good wage. There's no work for us, and no one will buy our cotton, anyhow, since the mill sells at prices we can't offer."

Isaac leaned forward. "It comes down to this. Close the mill, or we'll starve."

"You think you can bargain?" Her father's voice was too angry and loud. "You will all be hanged for this. Attacking a peer. Threatening the family. This is anarchy!"

Margot turned to glare at her father. "Mind your tongue, Lord Eastley. I am interested in solving this problem, and I will not see anyone hanged over it."

"This is not about you, Margot. This is not about Wickhamshire. This is about the very order of our society. You cannot upend it by listening to these…thugs. Your Grace, speak some sense into her."

Margot turned to Fitz. The Diplomatic Duke stood silhouetted in the drawing room window, moonlight setting his hair silver, the hearth lighting his gaze with fire. He stood for the realm; created and upheld the laws; molded the economy to encourage the order her father loved. As much as he might believe in her, as a duke, he might demand that she stop.

She would understand. She wouldn't obey, but she would understand.

"There will be repercussions felt across the country, to be sure, whatever the outcome," Fitz said, his eyes on her. Then he turned to her father. "However, this *is* about Wickhamshire. It is about these men and their families. Lady Wickham has a duty to solve it as she sees fit. Perhaps you and I should go see to the children."

It was in that moment, as he frog-marched her father from the room, that Margot realized she loved Fitz. No matter what had happened before or would happen after, she loved him, from the tip of his hair to the core courage of his heart.

It didn't matter, not just then, but it was good to know.

She returned her attention to the men in her drawing room. They wore a myriad of expressions on their faces: fury, fear, horror, shock, indignation. She supposed it was a terrible thing, for a daughter to ban her father from a room, no matter whether you were a member of the peerage or a weaver.

Margot folded her hands into her lap to project a sense of calm. "As you can see, I am quite serious about your situation. It is a bit of a mess. The mill is, unfortunately, already an established part of our economy. It helps me keep from raising the rents and allows me to offer funds to your brother tradesmen who need investments in their businesses. Moreover, even if I were to close our mill, another would open nearby, and then another. Such is the way of progress. Yet I know you and your families. I have no interest in seeing you go hungry or lose your pride without your industry of choice. What say you? Will you stay in conversation with me to find a solution other than closing the mill?"

The expressions before her changed, showing flickers of despair, hope, and anger. She settled for watching Josiah and Isaac. They looked at the men around them, then to each other. Finally, they met her gaze.

"We'll stay."

Chapter Twenty-One

Given that a minor insurrection was occurring below their feet, the house resounded with a curious quiet. From his guard outside the nursery, Fitz could hear but a few nocturnal sounds. The grandfather clock at the top of the stairs ticked with each minute. Outside, an owl hooted. One of the children coughed in their sleep.

And, of course, Lord Eastley muttered under his breath.

The man was going to lather himself into a heart attack if he wasn't careful. His face – wreathed in wisps of blond hair so unlike Margot's – boiled red as he forgot to take breaths. In one respect, Fitz supposed he could see the paternal resemblance. Margot had, without a doubt, inherited her passionate outbursts from Winpole.

Not for the first time, Winpole whipped around to charge his anger at Fitz. "I don't understand how you can condone this. If she shuts down her mill because a few weavers *asked* her to, every man across England will start sieging the estates, demanding their every whim. It's unnatural. It's dangerous. It's unnaturally dangerous."

He'd already said as much to Fitz three times over, and Fitz had pushed back with logical arguments. Of course, if this were Margot erupting at him, Fitz would know better than to rely on logic. She always understood the logic; what she objected to was deeper, core emotions that his logic neglected.

Perhaps Fitz's mistake here was supposing Winpole immune to such deeper tides.

"Do you know what I find most striking?" Fitz replied, before the man could turn the corner on another rant. "That group of men came today with weapons. They planned to destroy this house. Instead, they are sitting down to tea."

"Because they are being coddled. They should be hanged, not invited into the drawing room!"

"Did you see the way Lady Wickham commanded that room?" Fitz pressed on. "I've never seen thirty men listen to one woman so attentively, let alone as she was preparing tea."

Winpole at least didn't have a rejoinder to this.

"It may not look like the control that you or I are used to having, Winpole, but Lady Wickham has full control over this situation, and I have faith she will find a solution that does not include closing the mill."

Inside the nursery, one of the children – Valentina, Fitz thought, from the sound of the voice – cried out. He and Lord Eastley froze, bracing for more. One of the men could have scaled the side of the house to abduct the children. But instead, Fitz heard Nurse's soothing murmurs, calming the child back to sleep.

Fitz leaned against the wall, exhaling his fear in one fell breath.

Winpole sank to the ground, resting his back and head

against the door frame. "When Margot arrived at Bleneccle Manor last fall, she could barely look after the little ones, let alone an entailment. Why, she didn't get out of bed that first week except on the Sabbath, when Sybil dragged her out to go to the service. There was no question about my stepping in for her." He sighed. "I came here to apologize, you know. For what was said. For not seeing that she had healed. But here I am again, charging around like a bull."

How Fitz hated the idea of Margot so helpless in grief. How he would hate to be the one responsible for it. Even if he married her, he would want her to stand on her own so that if he died first, she wouldn't collapse.

He discovered with a bit of unease that Winpole was now looking at him. That unease increased when the man said, "You're in love with my daughter, aren't you, Your Grace?"

There was nothing to do but to admit it. Fitz nodded.

Winpole didn't exactly smile. "It's not my business any longer whom she loves or how she loves them. However, for what it might be worth, I'd pick you, if I could."

"Thank you."

"Do you plan to make her an offer?"

Fitz cleared his throat. What a question. Marrying Margot. A beautiful bride she'd be, and a gracious duchess thereafter.

If only she weren't still in mourning. If only she didn't have a four-year-old heir to raise to his entailment.

If only she would take a husband, and if only that

husband could be Fitz.

"Yes," Fitz said, and it was only after he said it that he knew it had been his answer for days. No matter that it would mean bucking tradition and losing the wager to Talbot and Annabelle. He loved Margot. There was nothing else to consider.

"I don't know that she will accept, but I plan to ask her to marry me."

Chapter Twenty-Two

Margot couldn't sleep. Her body still burned with the thrill of the evening. She'd spent over an hour negotiating with the weavers, discussing everything from subsidizing the cost of materials to improving parish poor house conditions. Their final compromise was complicated in execution yet simple in concept. The mill would stay open, but the weavers would lease the looms and share in the profits.

Now the weavers were sleeping in her house – tucked into the guest rooms, the servants' quarters, even the barn. Margot had seen to each of them before retiring to the family wing. Her father and Fitz had been waiting outside the nursery, telling each other tales of King Arthur's knights to pass the time. Fitz had bid her goodnight quickly, but her father had lingered to help her check on the children.

After she pressed kisses to George and Valentina's slumbering foreheads, her father took her hand. "I will always want to help and protect you, but I see how I have been doing the opposite. I hope you can forgive me and have patience while I learn new ways."

They were good, solid words. Margot squeezed his hand to accept them. "I mean to bring change into this world. You won't always like it. You may even find yourself belittling me, or dismissing me as a powerless woman, or deciding that I have overexerted myself."

"I shall do no such thing," he protested. Margot let him keep his fantasy, for now.

"I warn you, I will not listen to you. But I promise you that I will love you and respect you, no matter what."

His face had turned red, the way it always did. She could tell he was about to argue, so she pressed a kiss to his cheek. "Sleep well, Papa."

With all that tumbling through her head, Margot couldn't imagine even closing her eyes, much less getting to sleep. Not even a book could capture her attention. All she could do was sit near the window and let her thoughts roam.

Last night at this time – had it only been one night ago? – she had retreated from Fitz's bedchamber, heart bleeding from the injury of his words. But he hadn't meant them. For the first time, the Duke of Diplomacy had let his emotions get the better of him, and she'd been the victim. Margot believed his apology, not only because of the way his heart leapt into his words but also because he had trusted her so completely all night. Fitz believed in her. Fitz stood back so she could make the decisions.

And she loved him for it.

The thought put a smile on her lips. She loved the Duke of Harrodshire.

Somehow, the knock at her door didn't surprise her. Margot knew before she even turned the knob that it was Fitz.

He still wore his evening clothes, down to the white gloves on his hands. She would do something about that, if he allowed it.

"May I help you, Your Grace?" she asked as he stepped into the room.

Fitz looked down at her with those warm, piercing eyes. "I'm here on multiple accounts. First, I commend you on a successful negotiation."

Margot grinned. "Thank you."

"Second, how are you? I found that all rather alarming. Perhaps you did too?"

Alarming was an understatement. Margot would have used the words frightful, terrifying, or horrifying. The window of her study was still smashed to pieces; smoking torches still lay on her driveway; and she supposed Josiah still had that rock tucked into his pocket, just in case.

But the worst of it was behind them. As long as she kept her side of the bargain, she trusted they would too.

"It was mildly distressing, I suppose," she responded to Fitz. "It should make for a good tale to tell George, don't you think? A real-life example of daring, danger, and diplomacy."

"A good story for Valentina, too. For once, a story where the heroine saves the day, while the hero looks on in awe."

What a nice idea. Margot decided to add that to her list: find more stories with heroines who did more than wait in a castle.

Fitz cleared his throat. He put his hand in his pocket and then took it out again. "There is a third reason for my visit."

Margot smiled again to put him at ease. "I hoped there was. Perhaps I can guess at what it is."

But he didn't take her bait for seduction. Instead, Fitz knelt before her and took her palm in his. "I have come to realize I will never be satisfied with a mere friendship. I'm not sure when, but you have claimed my heart. You are beautiful, intelligent, caring, and everything I wish for in a wife. Would you do me the honor of becoming my duchess?"

Margot had never expected such a declaration. Fitz's hand was strong around hers, his eyes bright and hopeful, and she wanted nothing more than to say yes.

She joined him on the floor, pressing her lips to his for a delicious kiss. She would love to be his wife. They would host parties in London to sway the *ton* towards progress; they would find new practices in the country that bolstered their people instead of destroying them. Fitz would make her his partner; that much Margot knew.

But she couldn't say yes. Not yet. There was too much here in Wickhamshire that needed mending. She couldn't leave her weavers at the moment of their deal, no more than she could abandon the mill workers who deserved an indoor lunchroom. And that was what she had uncovered in her first afternoon back. Margot could only imagine what else needed her attention, now that she could give it.

Ending their kiss, Margot cradled Fitz's face between

her palms. He was so handsome, so perfect. "Would you accept a compromise?"

His eyes widened in surprise. "What do you have in mind?"

"I'm needed here, at least until I can put things to rights and set the county on a course of success. In the meantime, will you accept me as your promised bride?" Margot lowered her hands to catch his. "We would write each other. Visit each other. Once I'm out of mourning, you could squire me around town if we're in London together. Then, when the time is right, we marry."

For a moment, Margot wasn't sure Fitz would accept it. Why should he? He needed a wife to bear him heirs, not an independent friend.

But then he smiled. It was the most glorious smile Margot had ever seen, wide and true and sparkling, even in the dimmest candlelight.

"You have a deal, my Diplomatic Duchess."

Epilogue

Two Years Later

June spread its arms around Wickhamshire with a smile; yellow daisies painted the fields, warbling goldfinches dotted the skies, and good food filled everyone's bellies. Rosebushes bloomed at either side of the church door, and wreaths of larkspur and white snapdragons hung on the kissing gates. Folk from across the county were gathering, all in their Sunday best, all chattering about the luck of a beautiful wedding day.

The bride and groom, however, were running late.

For one thing, they were supposed to be in separate drawing rooms awaiting their carriages with bated breath. Instead, they were locked together in the study.

For another, they were supposed to have finalized their marriage contract weeks ago, yet here they were, debating the final points.

In her fine gown – the color of lemon with white rosebuds embroidered along the trim – Margot sat behind the desk, while Fitz lounged in the chair opposite, his long legs stretched lazily towards his bride.

"I'll grant you the provision that we spend equal amounts of time in the summer at each property, but I won't commit to two weeks," Fitz was saying.

Margot raised a fierce eyebrow. "Why not?"

"What if one year a storm hits Wickhamshire and we need to stay here longer? I don't want to feel that we must leave simply because of a clause in our marriage contract."

Margot did not miss how he used the property *she* cared most about as the example. Even after all this time, she had so much still to learn from Fitz, about negotiating and otherwise.

"Fine." She raised her chin, as if ceding the point were a favor to him. Then – because she couldn't help herself – she abandoned her seat in exchange for depositing herself squarely on his lap. She reveled in his smiling gray gaze as she leaned in for a sinful kiss.

"For shame, madam," Fitz whispered against her cheek. "We're not yet married!"

"That did not give you pause last night," she teased back. The fire that lit across his face was more than enough of a reward. Margot wriggled in her seat.

"I see what you're doing." Fitz's voice grew thick. "You will not win your extra month of honeymooning through seduction. I'm not so base as to forget my obligations to Parliament simply because a pretty woman bats her eyelashes at me."

"Ah, but you forget. I'm not merely a pretty woman, and I'm doing much more than batting my eyelashes." To prove her point, Margot trailed a finger down the long expanse of his chest.

"Pixie." Fitz caught her hand and brought it up to his

lips for a kiss. "Still, I must be in town to see through the national schools bill. And *you* must be here to oversee the installation of the new looms."

Margot knew it was true. Fitz was as passionate about his national schools agenda as he had been about the apothecary bill, which had been enacted as law the year before. He would be in his element in London, working in the name of a better England. And in the name of making sure her beloved little dominion was healthy, Margot would be in her element in Wickhamshire.

If she had learned anything over the last two years, it was that their life would never be stagnant. Fitz had new goals every six months, it seemed, as national interests shifted. Margot's aspirations were more fixed, yet no less heady. She had helped guide Wickhamshire to a new, steadier economy; she had started a school for the local girls; in London, she and Annabelle cosponsored a salon for ladies to debate politics.

But while she and Fitz moved in parallel directions, Margot didn't fear he would ever set her aside for his passions. Even when they were apart, she knew his every thought, fear, and feeling. And he knew hers.

It was, she believed, what had fueled them to so much success thus far.

A clamor of voices outside the study roused Margot from her musing. For the past week, Corinium Park had been overtaken with guests, including her whole family and the Talbots. George and Valentina adored having their cousin Cordelia visit. As for Margot, she would enjoy the company more if she didn't long for privacy with Fitz.

"I suppose we are being rude," she sighed, sliding from Fitz's lap.

"Annabelle is growing anxious that we have decided not to marry after all," Fitz smiled, "in the name of one hundred pounds."

In the hall, Lord Eastley bellowed, probably from impatience, followed by a murmur of assurance from her mother and Alice.

Standing, Fitz removed a paper from his jacket pocket and handed it to Margot. "Given that we are horribly late, may I present one final clause?"

"Clause M," Margot read. That was enough to trigger another raised eyebrow. "We only have Clauses A-F. Or are there hidden ones all the way through L that I'm not aware of?"

"M for Margot." Fitz gave her a wink. How her heart tripped whenever he did that. "This one is especially for you."

Margot skimmed the passage, then returned and read it more carefully. She looked up to Fitz – her handsome, perfect, soon-to-be husband – with a smile trembling on her lips.

"The right to revisit and amend this contract at any time, anywhere, for any reason."

He moved to her side. "You are my partner. And, if you don't delay us any longer, you'll be my wife. Before the honeymoon ends, I'm sure you'll have more ideas for how this partnership should look. I'll never be uninterested in hearing them."

Margot would never be uninterested in him. She claimed a long, delicious kiss as the final stamp of negotiation. Then she took his hand. "Let's sign this contract already, so we can get married."

Thank you for reading!

Every single reader makes me giddy. I hope you enjoyed *The Duchess Wager* as much as I enjoyed writing it!

If you can, please take a moment to leave a review on Goodreads, Amazon, BookBub, or wherever you like to share your thoughts on books.

As an independent author, I rely on reviews from readers like you to fuel my marketing. There's nothing more powerful than one reader hearing what another liked or didn't like.

Speaking of the internet, let's keep in touch. Come find me on social media or sign up for my newsletter for book recommendations, raffles, and sneak peeks:

- Sign up for my newsletter at www.katherinegrantromance.com

- Follow me on Instagram at www.instagram.com/katherine_grant_romance

- Like my page on Facebook at https://www.facebook.com/ katherinegrantromanceauthor

If you enjoyed this book, read on for an excerpt from the first book in the Countess Chronicles Series, Alice and Hugh's story: *The Ideal Countess*.

Historical Note

The Luddite Rebellion was a major series of protests and riots during the Regency era. For centuries, weaving had been a good vocation with steady work, good pay, and protection through guilds. Then, starting in the mid-1700s, technology like the spinning jenny, spinning mule, and steam looms introduced mass-production. Suddenly, a rich man could open a factory, hire unskilled workers and children, and sell a lot more cotton at a much lower price than the weavers could.

The weavers who found themselves out of work protested. They started with petitions; in February 1811 (a month after *The Duchess Wager* takes place), weavers in Bolton even petitioned the Prince Regent for economic relief. When the petitions didn't work, they started attacking the machines and mill owners' homes. They were called Luddites because they followed a legendary figure, Ned Ludd (who is generally believed to be a myth).

If you would like to learn more about the Luddites, I recommend:

Article:

"Luddism and Politics in the Northern Counties," by John Dinwiddy, from *Social History* Volume 4, published in 1979 (www.jstor.org/stable/4284859).

Blog Post:

"The Luddites," by Jessica Brain from Historic UK (https://www.historic-uk.com/HistoryUK/HistoryofBritain/The-Luddites/)

Podcast:

"Chapter 24: The Luddites," by Dave Broker from The Industrial Revolutions, published August 6, 2019 (https://industrialrevolutionspod.com/episodes/2019/8/6/chapter-24-the-luddites)

Each region had a Lord Lieutenant who mustered the militia, and by 1811, regiments were usually assigned to counties other than their home county (to reduce their sympathies with any insurrections). However, the militia probably wouldn't have been dismissed for the winter. If anything, they would be stationed in the town during the winter and leave for training in the summer. If you would like to learn more about the militia, I recommend:

Article:

"Sighing for a Soldier: Jane Austen and Military Pride and Prejudice," by Tim Fulford, from *Nineteenth Century Literature* Volume 57, published in September 2002.

Book:

Embodying the Militia in Georgian England, by Matthew McCormack, Oxford University Press, 2015

Finally, the road trip likely would have been a much bigger affair. There would have been at least one extra carriage with some more servants and necessary items, such as sheets (to avoid bedbugs). I hope you'll forgive me the liberty of forcing Margot and Fitz into a carriage together.

Acknowledgments

When I first started writing this book, I was still working full-time as a marketer and squeezing my author life into the weekends. I made Margot my alter-ego to talk myself into taking a leap of faith. I needed to gather my hopes and dreams and fears and use them to launch myself forward, and I embodied that story with Margot.

It was really scary. I couldn't have done it without my amazing husband, Michael. He enthusiastically agreed that quitting my day job was the right move. When I kept chickening out, he pestered me about it, asking if I'd quit yet. And now he celebrates all my successes and supports me through my fears. He also does all the cooking! Really, how did I get so lucky?

My sister Sarah (PhD) has been my number one fan since I finished my first unpublished novel in 2003, and she continues to be the very first person to see my projects. I rely on her for thoughtful feedback as well as fangirling. Thank you for being my unpaid beta reader!

My parents have encouraged my writing my whole life. As I make myself into an author, they have provided copy editing, critical feedback, word-of-mouth marketing, and love and support. Thank you so much for making room for my dreams!

Thank you to the professionals who helped make this book a product: my editor Jenny Proctor at Midnight Owl Edits (who rightfully points out that I use a lot of colons!) my copy editor Sara Israel, my amazing cover designer Julia Gerbach, and the gracious Asya Blue who calmly answers all my questions as she puts it into layout.

There are dozens of people on the periphery who keep me encouraged. My extended family, including my Aunt Katherine who is my most loyal social media follower, and my family-in-law, who are my word-of-mouth powerhouses. My writing friends, including Allison Manley, Kira Frank, and Jen Trinh. My #bookstagram friends, especially Melissa Makarewicz (@probablyatthelibrary). And every reader who takes the time to review the book, or shares their copy with a friend, or simply enjoys my books. You make it possible for me to live a life of joy!

Excerpt from
The Ideal Countess

The Duchess Wager is the second full novel in the Regency Romance series, The Countess Chronicles.

The full Countess Chronicles series includes:

The Ideal Countess

Midnight kisses. Fast gavottes. Secret duels. Alice Winpole just wants a successful Season, but she gets so much more.

New Year's Masquerade

Bernard Talbot is one day away from marrying Miss Lisbeth Dawes when his long-lost love, the Duchess of Surrey, returns as a widow. Caught between duty and happiness, Bernard must decide what will be the right step for his future.

The Duchess Wager

Fitz, the Duke of Harrodshire, views marriage as a business arrangement, not a question of the heart. Especially once he bets his friends that he won't marry the next woman he fancies. He knows it will be an easy win - until he meets Lady Margot Wharton.

Countess Chronicles #3 – Coming Soon

Lisbeth Dawes doesn't make the same mistake twice, which is why she has decided to marry a man sight unseen.

Keep reading to enjoy the first chapter from *The Ideal Countess!*

Chapter One

Miss Alice Winpole's first ball was almost everything she had dreamed it would be.

There was the footman at the door, bellowing ancient family names so she could peer over at the viscounts and barons and even one duke as they entered. There was the string quartet in the corner that never played a note out of tune, unlike the overeager fiddlers her mother hired for their country parties; the instrumentalists featured an olive-toned violinist who Alice was sure had been imported straight from Milan. There were ladies swathed in precious silks and gentlemen in their richest suits. Couples young and old slipped through double doors for fresh air on the Romanesque patio. Alice's mother had even whispered that there were orange-flavored ices in the refreshment room.

For a first ball, it was surpassing all of Alice's expectations, which were quite considerable since she'd been hearing about the splendor of the Season for the entirety of her seventeen years. The ball was perfect, in every way except one.

Alice had not yet been asked to dance.

Her parents, the Baron and Baroness of Eastley, had coached her on this. For the exact same amount of time that Alice had been hearing about balls, she had also been happily ensconced in their country seat of Bleneccle Manor. While her father undertook the five-day journey to London a few times a year, it was far too long—and far too likely that a coach wheel would break and the ladies would be stranded in a one-room inn—for him to invite the family along. Her mother had warned Alice that since they were so remote in their corner of the north, it would take a few weeks to properly introduce Alice so that gentlemen *could* ask her to dance. Alice had been fully prepared to stand against the wall during her first ball for one or two dances.

But things were not going according to plan. Alice and her mother were supposed to have arrived a full week before this first ball of the season, thrown by the Marchioness of Leighstor, so that her mother could take Alice around on morning calls to meet the matrons of society. But first a wretched rainstorm had delayed the start of their journey by two days, and then on the highway through Nottinghamshire a carriage wheel *did* break. The carriage-maker in town was laid up with what Lady Eastley called an unmentionable disease, so they had to wait another two days for the fix. By the time Alice set eyes on London – loud, messy London – there had been barely enough time to present her to the queen much less anybody else.

And so, Lady Eastley and Lord Eastley had deposited Alice against the very wall where she still stood before melting into the crowd to find her some dance partners. Playing the part of Marriage Mama, Lady Eastley chatted with fellow matrons, angling for introductions to their sons or nephews or brothers in hopes she could then introduce said gentlemen to Alice. Lord Eastley, meanwhile, had decamped to the cluster of males in the card room, promising to send every eligible male her way.

Alice had more faith in her father. While Lady Eastley was pretty and polite, she didn't have many connections, and she far preferred chatting over tea to rubbing elbows with London's *ton*. In the ballroom, she was being relegated to the quietest of conversation circles. In contrast, Lord Eastley knew more people in London, and he was the type of friendly boisterous that made people want to like him. Many times at home, Alice had observed a tenant or laborer come to Papa with a complaint, only for the man to leave laughing with a compromise as a solution.

Yet despite her parents' efforts, the caller had already announced the first minuet, a quadrille, and a polka, and Alice remained with no introductions. She glanced at her dance card as fellow debutantes walked arm-in-arm with gentlemen to start the polka. At the start of the evening, she'd written her name at the top in her brightest lettering, excited to see the card fill up. Now there were only eight more dances until supper, and every line was still blank. Indeed, the card itself was beginning to shrivel from all her fidgeting. Soon there wouldn't be a way for gentlemen to claim a dance, even if they wanted to.

Alice peeked at her fellow wallflowers. There were five or six others lined against the wall. At first, Alice had tried to make conversation with them – in truth, tried to make friends with them – but apparently the fate of the wallflower insisted on no conversation. The other ladies were almost all older than her, one of them surely over twenty, and wore dim colors or long faces. The one farthest from Alice had even pulled out some knitting. Surely in her new peach-pink gown, Alice stood apart. She kept her body angled toward the dance floor, a hopeful yet demure expression on her face. Certainly, any observer must see that she didn't belong with the wallflowers. Soon she would have an introduction, which would lead to another, and before she knew it, she would be the talk of the town.

If she'd been back at Bleneccle Manor, this wouldn't be a problem. Even if no one asked her to dance, Alice would simply march up to an available gentleman and ask him herself. But in London, everything was different. She was here as a member of peerage, to find a husband of good standing, and so she would act every part a lady.

The polka came to an end. Alice tried to look happy for the dancers as they laughed and clapped and turned to their next partners. There was absolutely no way under any circumstance that she would acknowledge the knot in her stomach, the one that got bigger and sorer every second she remained unnoticed. She was the daughter of Lord Reginald Winpole, Baron of Eastley, and she had no feelings except pleasant ones. In fact, even if the whole ball passed and she spoke to no other soul, she was determined to enjoy it.

Alice was so set on enjoying the ball that she didn't even notice a man approaching until he was right beside her.

"Miss Alice, what a delight to see you here this season."

Lord Hugh Osborne, Earl of Windemere, their neighbor to the south by twenty miles, bowed before her.

Somehow, instead of jumping out of her skin in surprise, Alice managed a responding curtsy, as if she spoke to gentlemen at balls all the time. Of course, she *had* spoken to Lord Windemere at balls before, since he was always invited to Lady Eastley's Christmas balls. She had spoken to his lordship at meals, too, and on horse rides and even one time shared a coach with him and his mother.

A few years older than she, Lord Windemere was the type of boy who barely saw past his own glasses. He was always reading a book or sketching inventions on spare paper. The last time she had seen him – a few years ago, before he went off to Cambridge – all he could talk about was his belief that England could prevent a revolution if only they invented new farm tools. Terrible Alice, in fact, had wished him well at university and whispered as he'd walked away, "Don't come back!"

Yet now, Lord Windemere was the best thing she had ever seen. His hair was longer, the color of chestnut and curling as a frame to highlight a sculpted face: sloping cheekbones, slender nose, and eyes that were a piercing blue even through his thick round spectacles. He seemed to have grown a few inches, too, and his shoulders were thicker, stronger. In her haze of gratitude, Alice found him so handsome that her breath caught at the base of her throat.

He was commenting something about the ball, and she completely missed it. She smiled to make up for it. Lord Windemere's eyes darted to the blank card in her hand. "Do you by any chance have this quadrille available?"

Alice blushed. "Yes, thank you."

He took her hand to lead her to a place in the dance line. His grip was firm yet gentle through the kid skin gloves they both wore. Alice wondered if she would notice how every gentleman led her to the floor, of if she was only so aware because this was her first dance in London. When they reached their respective places across from one other in the two lines, Hugh winked at her, and Alice blushed again.

The quadrille was not Alice's favorite dance. At home, she preferred the galop because it required such energy to leap from one foot to the next. The quadrille was too stately, less of a dance than a choreographed walk. But as the violin played its first chords and the caller announced the first steps, she began to appreciate the careful tempo. At Bleneccle Manor, Alice had no need for conversation. Here at the marchioness's ball, the quadrille gave her every excuse to speak not only to Hugh but also to the other dancers. Between Hugh's polite questions about their journey and how long they planned to be in London, she was passed to an earl, a baron, and a viscount. She overheard *their* conversations with their partners. The earl even asked who her father was, which nearly promised an introduction later. It wasn't a dance at all, and yet she finished just as breathless as if she'd done a jig.

Lord Windemere claimed her hand again. He led her not to the wallflowers but to her mother, who was in a throng near the front, chatting with their hostess, Lady Leighstor. "Oh Lord Windemere, how clever of you," Lady Eastley exclaimed. "I didn't know you were here, otherwise I would have said good evening much sooner."

"It was a surprise to myself as well," Lord Windemere said. "Made even more pleasant when I discovered that my favorite neighbors are in attendance. I hope you don't mind, but I did impose on Miss Winpole for a quadrille."

Lady Eastley beamed, first at him, then at Alice. "That's so kind of you. I know she has quite been looking forward to dancing."

Alice's smile tightened. *Why* did her mother have to make her sound so pathetic? Lord Windemere had already found her in the bouquet of wallflowers. There was no need to hammer home the point that no one else had asked her.

Lord Windemere surprised her by turning back in her direction. "In that case, perhaps I can have the upcoming galop as well? If I recall, it is your favorite of the London dances."

Blinking, Alice tried very hard not to be speechless. Her mind raced to understand how Lord Windemere could possibly know what her favorite dance was, much less make the distinction between the fashionable dances and her true favorite, the regional jigs that would never be allowed in a London ballroom. If she opened her mouth, she would sputter, rather than give the gracious "I'd be delighted" that she *wanted* to say.

Before she could align her brain with her mouth, Alice was surprised again, this time by her father clapping a hand on Lord Hugh's shoulder. "Pleasure to see you, Windemere, but I'm afraid Miss Winpole's galop is spoken for."

Lord Windemere stepped back, making way for Lord Eastley to join the group. And *he* made room for yet another addition, a man Alice had noticed the moment he'd been announced to the ball. Tall, muscled under his silk coat, dark of hair and eyes and expression.

The Duke of Cornwall.

Even Alice, who knew nothing about the *ton*, had heard of the duke. He'd just returned from the West Indies, where it was whispered he saved ten men in a battle to subdue local rebels. That he was an eligible duke had gotten everyone at the ball in a dither.

And now Alice's own father had secured an introduction.

"May I present my daughter, Miss Alice Winpole, Your Grace?"

The duke bowed over her hand, lifting his gaze to hers only as his lips met her glove. She felt the kiss as if it were a sear into her skin.

"At your service, my lady. When I saw you dancing so divinely with Osborne here, I knew I had to claim a figure for myself."

His words thrilled against her skin as surely as if he had touched her. Alice curtsied, smiled, tried not to show how flattered she was. Vaguely, she heard the musicians strike the opening chords.

"I believe that music is ours," the duke said. Even his voice was low, a bass thrill through Alice's body. She followed him to the dance floor. His grip was much stronger than Lord Windemere's, a vise around her hand that said he never wanted to let go. Alice quite lost her head: the Duke of Cornwall himself held her hand. Looked her in the eyes. Made her heart thump dangerously.

As the dance started – as her deepest fantasies of a ball in London came true – it was only in the back of Alice's mind that she registered Lord Windemere exiting the room, hat and greatcoat in hand.

Buy *The Ideal Countess* from your favorite bookstore to find out what happens next!